Stroke

Kaye George

An Imogene Duckworthy Mystery
Book 4

White City

Press

Also by Kaye George

A People of the Wind Mystery

Book 1
Death in the Time of Ice

Book 2
Death on the Trek

Book 3
Death in the New Land

Imogene Duckworthy Mysteries
Book 1
Choke

Book 2
Smoke

Book 3
Broke

Book 4
Stroke

ADVANCE PRAISE FOR BROKE

"I loved it. The series gets better and better."

—E. B. Davis, Short Story Writer, Avid Reader and Beach Bum

PRAISE FOR CHOKE

"A total delight! Laugh-out-loud dialogue, adorable characters, and a truly original voice. Fresh, feisty and hilarious. More, please."

—Hank Phillippi Ryan Anthony, Agatha and Macavity winning author

PRAISE FOR SMOKE

"A Texas-sized slice of murder and mayhem, makes for a fun, fast-paced read."

—Rhys Bowen, Agatha and Anthony-winning author of the Molly Murphy and Royal Spyness series.

"Kaye George knows how to write a fun mystery! She will make you laugh. Don't miss Smoke.

—Sasscer Hill, Agatha and Macavity Finalist

Stroke

Kaye George

Copyright © Kaye George 2023
White City Press Edition: 2024
White City Press is a division of Misti Media LLC
https://whitecitypress.com
Cover Design—Karen Phillips
Cover Design © 2023 Karen Phillips & White City Press
Available in both Paperback and eBook Editions
1 2 3 4 5 6 7 8 9 10
Paperback ISBN: 9781963479515
eBook ISBN: 9781963479492

Author's Note

As always, it has taken more than me, the author, to make this book happen. First of all, Jay Hartman for believing in me, and his White City Press for bringing it to publication. For detailed reads and edits: Kathy Waller, Jan Christensen, and Barry Fuller. For inspiration and encouragement: Peg Cochran and Marilyn Levinson. For my awesome cover: Karen Phillips of https://phillipscovers.com/.

Jan Christensen has been a faithful friend for a number of years and we've read each other's novels for errors, typos, timeline problems. Jan passed away suddenly March 18, 2023, and I must give her a special mention here and tell the world how much I miss her.

This book is dedicated to the late Heines, Linda and Virgil, and their dogs, who wanted their house and their dogs in one of my books.

One

"RALPH WILL BE...SO HAPPY I DID THIS. It sure is...heavy."

Imogene Duckworthy smiled and hummed as she panted and struggled, pushing Ralph's horrible old recliner onto the front porch of the stone house. When the ratty old thing was perching on the edge of the concrete porch slab, she dusted off her hands and looked up at the sky. A light snow was beginning to sift down. A few flakes fell on the dark brown cloth of the chair. They improved its lowly appearance, she thought.

She and her daughter now lived there with him. She smiled watching her daughter, Nancy Drew Duckworthy, playing in the front yard with Marshmallow, her pet potbelly. Drew would lob a tennis ball as high as thin, little arms could and the pig would retrieve it as well as any dog could. And without as much slobber.

Even though she never caught the name of the trucker who had inadvertently fathered Drew, she would always be grateful to him for giving her this gift.

Immy called them to come inside before they got soaked. It wasn't cold enough yet for the snow to stick, and the yard would be muddy if they kept running through it.

They all bundled into the living room. Drew shrugged off her medium-heavy jacket and let it drop to the floor.

"Where does that go, Drew?"

The four-year-old's smile pooched out her chubby, rosy cheeks and brought out her dimples. Immy couldn't help but lightly pinch her daughter's cheeks. Drew shrieked with mock horror and snatched her coat off the floor. Her motive probably had more to do with the fact that Marshmallow was heading toward it than her mother's order. Drew knew, from some past sad experiences, what a rooting pig could do to clothing. After hanging her jacket on a hook in the coat closet, she and the pig scampered into their bedroom.

Immy stood in the middle of the living room, holding her chin in one hand and cocking her head, envisioning her office in the corner, her desk up against the window, her plush chair positioned to see both the window and the front door, maybe a two-drawer filing cabinet beside the desk. No, a four-drawer would be better. She did not, currently, own any of these pieces of furniture.

But Immy was good at envisioning things. She had imagined herself as a full-fledged private eye for some time now. She even worked for one. Every day she pictured her name on the glass of her own office door: Imogene Duckworthy, Private Detective. When she got the certificate from the course she had just completed, she would frame it and hang it on the wall nearby.

While her mind was still pleasantly inside her imaginary office, Ralph Sandoval arrived with a bang, slamming the front door against the inside wall. Immy flinched at the sound and came back to earth.

"Immy, can you tell me why my chair is outside?" His jaw was tight and his teeth were gritted.

She hesitated. "Um, your chair? I took it out. It's old and ratty. Do you need it?"

"Need it? It's my favorite chair. It's where I unwind every day. Yes, Immy, I need it." He waved a sheaf of envelopes at her. He had obviously been to the post office to collect the mail on his way home from the Saltlick Police Station.

She swiveled, eyeing all the corners of the living room. It wasn't large. It held a comfy brown couch, the TV, a bookcase, a stereo cabinet, two end tables and two lamps. The space beside the window, where the recliner had been, was the only available place.

Immy set her hands on her hips. "Well, where is my desk going to go?"

"When did you get a desk?" Ralph dropped the mail onto an end table, shrugged his jacket off, and threw it onto the couch.

Immy didn't think it was a good time to remind him to hang it up. "I don't have one yet. But I have to have an office."

The look he gave her was slightly intimidating. As a cop, he was fairly adept at cold, steely glares. He propped the front door open with some old books from his bookcase and dragged his chair back to its corner. He swatted the snowflakes off the cloth surface. The next look he gave her made her shiver. Then he stalked into the bedroom.

Blinking back her tears, Immy plopped onto the couch. This was their first fight since she and Drew had moved in a week ago.

Before she could work herself into a good cry, the doorbell rang. Without waiting for anyone to answer the door, Immy's mother, Hortense Duckworthy, opened it and walked in. She, too, must have picked up her mail because she carried a small square envelope and the books Ralph had left outside.

"Imogene!" She handed the envelope to Immy. "Look what arrived today by postal delivery."

Immy blinked two more times and took it from her. The return address was Slap Out, TX. Where had she heard that before? "Should I open it? It's addressed to you, Mother."

"Yes, yes it is. But I want you to peruse the contents and give me your opinion. I have previously read the missive."

Immy slid the card out, dropping a thin piece of almost transparent paper. It landed in a wet spot on the floor, left by Ralph's boots. The card was a wedding invitation for the marriage of Loryetta Justice and Ned Newberry Jr. "Do we know them?"

"I know them, but you may not. The groom—"

"Geemaw!" Drew burst into the room and ran headlong to throw her arms around her grandmother's sturdy legs.

"Wait a moment, Nancy Drew. Let me compose myself." Hortense plopped into Ralph's recliner with an audible *oof*. She lifted her arms off the arm rests immediately, though. "This chair is wet."

"Well, yes," Immy said. "It was on the porch. It got snowed on."

"What is the reason for its having been on the porch? Did it need to be aired out?"

"It's a long story. Who are these people?" She held out the invitation.

Drew climbed into her grandmother's lap and rested her chestnut curls on Hortense's prodigious breast, nestling beneath her chins. Drew was used to her grandmother's ponderous manner of speaking. Hortense, a retired librarian, had a large vocabulary and believed in using it.

Marshmallow, not to be left out, trotted over to lie at Hortense's feet. When Immy looked closer, she realized Marshmallow was *on* her feet.

"Marshmallow," Immy said. "Get off Mother's—"

"Don't disturb his repose, Imogene. He is, to all appearances, comfortable. Now, to answer your inquiry, Ned Newberry, Jr., the groom, is the son of one of my female cousins."

"Have I ever heard of this cousin?"

Hortense studied the corner of the ceiling. "You have not."

When she didn't continue, Immy prompted her. "Why have I not heard of her? Is she a jailbird? A felon?"

"Such coarse language, Imogene. Please endeavor to elevate your lexicon. My cousin Ouida, is above reproach, except in her choice of a matrimonial partner. Ned Newberry, is a reprobate. Unfortunately, your father and I—rest his dear, departed soul—chose to sever relations with both of them many years ago. I have not seen Ned's name in a newspaper or on a televised broadcast for many years, so perhaps he has mended his egregious ways and it is time to reconcile. I have always felt sympathy for poor, wretched Ouida, though no amount of my attempted persuasion could induce her to come to her senses and leave the horrible man in the hole he had dug for himself."

"What's so horrible about him?"

"He is reputed to have swindled ranchers, through real estate transactions for land, out of not only land, but their rightful mineral rights, as I understand it."

"That's low. Poor dumb ranchers."

"The ranchers are not necessarily mentally deficient, Imogene. Some are merely uneducated or, even worse, trusting." Hortense looked around the room, slightly disturbing Drew's curls when her topmost chins brushed against the child's head. "Where is Ralph? I assume he has returned since his vehicle is parked in the driveway."

"I'm right here." Ralph strode into the room, nodded at Hortense and ruffled Drew's curls when she lifted her head to greet him with a smile. He ignored Immy. "Are you enjoying that chair?"

"It is slightly damp, but comfortable and sturdy."

"Yep. It's a great chair." He pressed his lips together. Immy thought that made his wide, strong face look even more masculine. "Not everyone appreciates a chair like that."

Immy couldn't keep still any longer. "Some people appreciate furniture that looks nice and isn't worn out." In spite of Ralph's glare, she kept going. "Some people would like to be treated decently and would like space to set up a home office."

"Oh dear." Hortense shooed Drew off her lap and hoisted her considerable weight out of the chair by pressing on the damp armrests. "I guess I will be taking my departure now. I can leave this missive here and you two can discuss whether or not you would like to accompany me. I would appreciate the companionship."

"Wait, Mother—"

"Hortense, don't—"

She ignored both of them and swept from the room, letting herself out the front door.

"Now look what you did," Immy said.

Ralph gave her a silent stare for a few seconds. "I see exactly what I did. I asked you to move in with me because you couldn't stand to live with your mother anymore. Your mother, who is a sweet person and a terrific cook. I remember that you jumped at the chance. And now I see that you have repaid me by trying to destroy my favorite chair."

"I…I'm very glad to be here, Ralph. I love living here. I love *you*. We can talk about where to put my office, okay?" Immy's stomach turned at the thought of how upset Ralph was. If she had had any idea he thought so much of that old chair…

"That would be sensible, wouldn't it? Instead of shoving my chair out of the house, into the weather."

"OK, I'm sorry I did that. I didn't know you were so attached to a ratty…to that—"

"Immy, what's this that you mother left here?" Ralph picked up the fancy envelope.

"It's a wedding invitation. Her cousin's son is getting married. It's very soon. Saturday." This was Thursday.

Ralph pulled out the stiff card and looked at it. "In Slap Out? That's down south of Dallas. Is Hortense going?"

"I think she wants to. She wants us to go with her."

Ralph remained still for another few moments, then tossed the invitation back onto the end table. "You go ahead. I'll stay here and see if I can find someone to get the damp smell out of my chair."

Two

After Ralph stomped out and drove off, saying he needed to do something at the station. Immy felt the tears welling up in her eyes. She sank onto the couch. It was, at least, dry.

"Mommy sad?" Drew climbed up beside her and laid her head on Immy's upper arm.

"Oh, sweetie, I just don't like to fight with Uncle Ralph."

"Well, don't fight then."

With that settled, Drew went to the bedroom she shared at night with the pig to entertain herself, something she was very good at.

After a couple of minutes, Immy crept into the bedroom she shared with Ralph and pulled open the top drawer of the dresser he had given to her. She drew out one of her most prized possessions, wrapped in an old, soft hanky. Sitting on the bed, she opened the small bundle and exposed the police detective badge that her father had proudly worn. When she was stressed, it calmed and soothed her to run her fingers over the shiny metal part and remember him, and the life her family had had before his violent death, trying to interrupt a robbery.

Back then, as far as Immy knew, nothing bad touched the small family of three, she and her mother and father. They had had Immy rather late. Her thin, happy mother worked in the Saltlick Public Library, Immy walked to school every day, and her father was a tall, strong hero who would never die.

Her mother would always grieve the death of her handsome policeman husband. Hortense, now retired from the library and in her fifties, was still the vivacious, attractive woman she had been, just a lot heavier, with the pounds that her grief had put upon her.

Calm settled onto Immy's shoulders and stopped the jangling spiral in her mind.

Yes, she would create that kind of family for her daughter. She would create it with Ralph. They would, the three of them, create a happy family. That included a pig named Marshmallow.

But they would have to drive to the wedding without him. They would go and come back. It wouldn't take long. And she would make it up to Ralph. Maybe she could have the chair professionally cleaned. But she would ask him first. Communication was important. All of the advice columns said so.

She would even learn to cook like her mother and Ralph would love to eat whatever she made. Well, maybe that was going a little too far. She would never cook like her mother. Her mind plummeted back to reality.

"Drew, come here for a minute. We have to pack." She dragged the medium-sized suitcase from under the bed and started putting in her underwear.

Drew came running in, Marshmallow trotting behind her. "I need to take this." She thrust a well-worn cloth dolly at her mother. "Can Marshmallow go, too?"

"I'm afraid he'll have to stay behind with Uncle Ralph. They can have lots of fun together."

"Marshmallow will make him feel better."

"I'm sure he will." She looked at the handsome black swine with the striking white star in the middle of his forehead.

Marshmallow looked back at Immy with his clear, blue eyes and it seemed possible that maybe he would.

Three

Hortense, the last one in, settled into the van and they started out.

"Imogene, did I apprise you of my recent conversation with my cousin, Ouida Newberry?"

"The mother of the groom, right? No, I guess not."

"I have not conversed with her for a few years. But I'm happy to say she sounds like the Ouida I once knew, before she married that man. Perhaps a bit stressed about the upcoming nuptials. That is to be expected, I am sure. I am eager to see her and assess her situation after all these years."

They chatted with Drew about the places they were passing through. Small towns like Henrietta and Sunset.

When they were halfway to Slap Out, Drew started saying she was "starrrrving." They happened to be approaching a Tex Mex restaurant on the edge of the good-sized town of Mammoth, which they were passing through.

"We could stop here." She turned around with a questioning look at Drew. "What do you think?" She was driving, since Ralph had gotten all strong and silent and had actually carried through on his threat and stayed behind. A persistent sinking feeling had taken up residence in the pit of her stomach. This had been their first big fight since they moved in together. Well, the first big fight ever. She kept glancing at the cell phone in the cup holder, hoping Ralph would call and beg forgiveness. If he didn't, she might have to.

"What is this place?" Drew asked.

Hortense answered. "This medium-sized metropolis is called Mammoth, so named after the archeology of the area, whence was discovered the fossilized remains of a sizeable herd of the ancient mammals. They were overcome, it is theorized, by the flooding waters of—"

"No, Geemaw, I mean the rest'rant."

Immy told her it looked like a decent place to have lunch. "Would you like to eat here?" She pulled into the lot and parked.

Drew's eyes grew bright. Rather than answer, she unbuckled herself from her car seat and opened the door. They were traveling in Hortense's ancient green Dodge van, to accommodate the three of them, including Hortense, luggage, and some wrapped wedding gifts.

The smell of wonderfulness drifted into the car with the crisp autumn air as Drew scrambled out.

"Nothing smells like Tex Mex," Immy said.

"I agree, nothing smells better than Tex Mex," Hortense added.

Drew ran toward the door and they followed at a more civilized pace.

Seated at a table that was pushed up against the wall in a corner, with four generously sized chairs, big enough so that Hortense sat comfortably, with their jackets on the extra chair, they placed and got their orders quickly. The diner was less than half full. As Drew munched her crunchy tacos and Hortense dug into her huge bean burritos, Immy started on her nachos, admiring the décor. The walls were a soft blue, and heavy Mexican-style ceramic plates were hung on them, high above their heads, near the ceiling. Except for a couple of places where plates had obviously been previously, judging from the spacing of the others.

"Mother," Immy asked, "do you think some of those plates fell off the wall?"

Hortense glanced around, focusing on the spaces and the round bits of missing plaster where the hangers had been. "I would surmise so." Then, with a look of alarm, she raised her voice. "Immy, you are positioned directly beneath some of them."

Immy sat against the wall with Drew in the chair next to her. Hortense was across the table with their jackets on the chair that was next to the wall on that side.

"I am, aren't I? They're sure pretty." She gazed at them and chuckled, picturing one of the plates falling on her head.

*****

When Immy awoke, she was on the floor and everyone in the restaurant was standing above her, concern on all the faces. She heard a distant pounding, then realized it was inside her head. And her head hurt. A lot.

"Mommy, you're alive!" Drew flung herself onto Immy tearfully.

Hortense glanced heavenward with a look of relief. "Imogene, lie still. A medical professional will arrive shortly. An emergency team has been summoned."

Immy blinked, noting how that made her head hurt. "What happened? Where am I?"

"We are still in the Tex Mex eating establishment. You were felled by a descending, weighty piece of decorative ceramic art."

"Oh, a plate hit me?"

"Yes, Mommy, that plate fell and hit you on the head. You fell right on the floor and you were asleep." Drew clutched her mother more tightly, getting Immy's face wet. "I thought you might be dead." Immy wanted to wipe her child's tears, but movement, even the slightest thing, made the pain in her head worse. She noticed the chair she had been sitting in lay still tipped over on the floor, next to her.

The EMTs arrived just then, rushed to where Immy lay and knelt to poke and prod and assess her. One of them asked her easy questions about dates and fingers and the president, the other strapped a blood pressure cuff on her arm and clipped an oximeter to her finger.

When they were done, they handed Hortense a list of things to watch for, saying she had a mild concussion and would probably feel better in a week or two. That seemed like a long time to Immy.

"Are you sure you feel competent to operate the automobile?" Hortense asked, as they left and Immy headed for the driver's seat.

"I can see just fine." She would rather not drive right now, but she didn't want to put up with the tortoise pace of Hortense's driving. She wanted to get there today.

"Please, no radio," she said, when Hortense started reaching for the dashboard. "And Drew, could you play really quiet? Mommy's head will hurt if you're noisy." It would hurt anyway, but it would be worse with Drew's high-pitched voice asking her the usual incessant stream of questions.

They were getting close to Slap Out. Immy steered Hortense's green van onto the ramp for the turnoff from I-35 to Corsicana. Hortense had insisted on using her van because she was more comfortable in it than in Immy's small car. Hortense was also, Immy thought, more comfortable in the passenger seat with Immy driving all the way and her not driving at all. Immy didn't need her to, but she should maybe have at least offered.

Immy had done nearly two hundred miles and had about thirty to go. She veered southeast, onto the road to Slap Out. She blinked to keep her weary eyes in focus.

"Is *this* Fwap Out?" Drew asked from her car seat in the back.

"Not quite yet, sweetie," Immy said. "We're almost there."

"That's what you said last time, Mommy. And the other last time and the other last time."

"We need to transport ourselves a mere twenty miles farther, Nancy Drew, and we will have arrived at our destination."

"Fwap Out?"

"Yes, *SL*ap Out." Hortense exaggerated the *S* and the *L*.

Immy thought Drew liked saying her version of the word "slap."

"Will the people fwap us?"

"No one will slap anyone. We will all behave as the civilized, decent people we are."

Immy missed Ralph, even though they'd only been apart for three hours. It wasn't the three hours that separated them the most though, it was the two hundred miles. And that damn recliner. She had a hard time believing that anyone could value such a piece of crap. And he seemed to value it above Immy's feelings. That was the hard part.

True, she did have an inkling that maybe she had been in the wrong. Maybe she had acted impulsively. Maybe Ralph had a right to get upset with her, but not *this* upset. She would have felt so proud to show up in front of her mother's relatives on the arm of the big, strong, handsome Officer Ralph Sandoval. Even though she had never met any of these relatives, she knew they would be impressed.

Four

THE LAST FEW MILES WENT QUICKLY. It was pretty country, not all flat like the high plains of west Texas. The land rolled slightly and was dotted with small trees and brush. As they got into town, the trees increased in size. The houses were varied, from very small to almost plantation size, fronted by huge porches complete with massive pillars. Most of the large houses were in good shape. Not so for the smaller ones.

One of the first businesses they came to was a gas station, so she pulled in to ask for directions and advice on a place to stay.

An ancient man in overalls hobbled over to the van. "Regular?" he asked.

"Regular what?" she countered.

"Yer at a gas station." He gave her an odd look. "Regular gas. You want regular or high test?"

This man was going to pump the gas for her? People still did that? She might as well take advantage and let him fill her tank. "Uh, yes, regular, please."

Immy could have done it faster, but it was nice to have the man wait on her. He cleaned the bugs off the windshield, too. "Want your tires checked?"

She didn't think that would be necessary. "Could you direct me to the nearest motel?" she said as she handed him her credit card.

"Be right back." He doddered into the office where she could see him through the large, dirt-streaked plate-glass window swiping the card with an old-fashioned mechanical card reader. When he returned, he directed her to the other edge of town where, he said, was the motel, the *only* motel.

She drove down a main cross street and pulled into the Motel Four parking lot, trying to miss most of the potholes. The place must have been built when a room cost four dollars, she thought, and had never been updated since then.

"I wonder if there is a more respectable-looking establishment that we might try." Hortense gave a doubtful look at the weeds surrounding the dingy once-white building. An office was nearest the road, with the rooms stretching out in a line that marched away from it. "One which has not fallen on such obviously hard times."

"That man said this is the only one."

"Perhaps we could try a neighboring community."

"Mother, I looked online before we started out. The nearest town is thirty-five miles away. We're only going to be here a couple of nights."

"That is true, Imogene. We should be able to abide these conditions for two nights. We will not be spending long hours here."

The rehearsal dinner was slated to begin in an hour, so they unloaded their luggage into the small, dark room as soon as Immy had checked them in.

"What is that odor?" Hortense lifted her head and sniffed.

Drew imitated her, blowing out through her nose instead of in, her version of "smelling."

"There have been illicit chemicals here."

"I think it's more marijuana than meth."

"That is not particularly reassuring, Imogene."

"On second sniff, I don't think it's meth at all. Is that better?" She could detect body odor, for sure, and other body-related smells that she didn't want to think about too deeply.

"Incrementally, if we are using quite a small increment."

Immy hung her dress for the wedding tomorrow on a hanger in the closet after clearing out a few cobwebs. "I wonder when the last person stayed in this room. It's only for two nights."

"I will repeat that to myself a substantial number of times in an effort to draw comfort from those words." Hortense hung up her dress and Drew's.

Then they all set their suitcases onto the beds, opened them, and got into their rehearsal dinner clothes. Immy had a nice blue sweater that looked good with her new jeans and her blue boots. Drew wore a version of the same outfit, but with a red sweater and boots. Hortense wore her best muumuu, which had a swirly blue-green-gold pattern. It did nothing to minimize her size, but Immy didn't think she was interested in doing that.

Drew was dressed first, probably because others dressed her, then dressed themselves, as usual. She wandered off and busied herself by poking around the place.

Immy went into the bathroom to carefully apply her eye makeup and try to keep it off her sweater.

Luckily, the mascara wand was not near her face when she heard a noise like a banshee. She realized her mother had screamed. She had never heard that before.

"Mommy, come look!"

She ran to the bedroom where Hortense and Drew were regarding a bed with the covers pulled back.

"I found lots and lots of cute little bugs. Aren't they cute?"

Hortense was backed into the corner, soundlessly pointing at the bared bed.

Immy peered at the bed.

"Aw, they ran away. They're hiding."

They had not disappeared completely, though. Immy could see trails of little black dots, which she had to assume were their leavings.

"Imogene, we cannot domicile here tonight."

"You're right, Mother. But it's time to go. Let's figure out something after the rehearsal dinner."

"Nancy Drew, close up your suitcase and fasten it completely."

"Good idea, Mother. Let's put everything into the car. We probably shouldn't come back here. Good thing I only paid for one night."

After moving out of the motel, they climbed into the van to attend the festivities, as Hortense called them.

Immy consulted her GPS for directions to the church, which was only a few blocks away, given that the town was about ten blocks by fifteen. Her mouth fell open when they pulled into the parking lot beside the edifice.

The church looked like it belonged in a huge metropolis. It was a grand building, with wide steps in the front and turrets at the corners, giving it a faintly Moorish look. However, the rehearsal dinner seemed to be in the metal prefab building across the parking lot. The church was dark, except for an outside light, but the other building was brightly lit and most of the cars were clustered on that side of the lot.

"I think we're here," Immy said, unnecessarily.

"We're in Fwap Out?" Drew asked.

"Yes, Nancy Drew, this is still officially Fwap…Slap Out." Hortense smiled when she corrected herself.

"It's not like the Motel Four," Immy said. "This is a different part of town."

"Much different, fortuitously."

The three of them entered a room that took up most of the large structure. An open kitchen area, separated from the main room by a counter, occupied one end, along with restrooms. Long folding church tables were spread with white cloths and set with blue candles in glass holders. Most of the people milled about while a few women scurried back and forth from the kitchen to the buffet tables along one wall, laden with heaps of delicious smelling meats, a few vegetables, and large pies and cakes.

At the far end of the room, a band banged away at something. Immy couldn't pick out what they were attempting to play, but she gave them credit for using a lot of volume, especially the young female drummer.

The lights in the room were dim, but someone had set up strobe lights beside the musicians, shining out on the guests and making their faces alternately blue, green, red and yellow.

"People still use strobe lights?" Hortense said, leaning close to Immy's ear to be heard.

Immy shrugged. "*These* people do."

Hortense picked out her cousin, Ouida Newberry, helping to carry dishes out of the kitchen area. "It seems odd that the groom's mother is made to wait tables. I desire to converse with her for a moment, at least."

She headed for her cousin, a small, dried-up looking woman dressed in dark maroon slacks and a white blouse, who wore her dark, gray-streaked hair in a tight bun at her nape.

Immy stayed fairly close to the door they had entered through with Drew, who held her hand with an iron grip. There were no other small children, so Drew was probably intimidated. Immy tried to pick out the bride and groom. The bride was easy. She was still in her veil, tossed back over her head and hanging down her back. It was a long veil. She had no doubt worn it for the rehearsal, but Immy thought that, if it were her, she would have taken it off by now. She didn't have on her wedding gown, of course, but wore blue jeans and a pale pink shirt. The groom was probably the uncomfortable-looking man standing stiffly at her side, looking away from the people crowded about his intended, smiling at her and kissing her on the cheek sporadically. Immy realized he was glaring at the band. Maybe he was a musician and didn't appreciate the lack of talent.

An older man standing nearby spoke to her. "Don't know why Eccles couldn't spring for a country band." He shook his head violently, apparently trying to clear the racket out of his ears. His cowboy hat hunkered solidly on his curly gray hair, not moving at all.

"Who is Eccles?" Immy asked.

"Eh?"

She raised her voice to be heard. "I asked who Eccles is."

The man pointed a work-worn hand at a man near the bride. "Loryetta's daddy. Father of the bride. Cheap bastard."

Eccles Justice wore a sport coat and jeans and large round glasses, his suspiciously dark hair slicked straight back. He was a small, tidy man.

Immy didn't like the mean sneer on the nearby man's face and started to move away with Drew. But he extended the hand he'd pointed with and introduced himself.

"The name's Harbor. Sydney Harbor. Pleased ta meetcha."

Immy shook his calloused, warm hand. "Yes, same here." Then she skedaddled with Drew. She found herself at the end of the buffet table, so she took two plates and started filling them, following the line of people doing the same. As she reached the end of the table, she looked around for a place for her and Drew to sit. About half the seats were empty. Card tables were scattered around, among the long, rectangular tables, and set at angles that she imagined must be artistic. They held wrapped gifts that someone had bothered to arrange nicely.

She set the two plates at one empty table and leaned a chair forward to save a place for her mother.

"Hello. I don't believe I know you." The bride with her veil was suddenly next to them.

Immy let go of Drew's hand to shake the bride's. Drew snatched it back as soon as the clasp ended. "I'm Imogene Duckworthy. My mother is a cousin of Ouida, your groom's mother, right?" Immy looked toward the two women, who stood nodding and talking to each other outside the kitchen. It looked like they were having a cordial reunion.

"Oh yes. I'm Loryetta Justice, soon to be Loryetta Newberry." Her smile looked tentative to Immy, who wondered if the bride was having doubts.

"Yes, tomorrow," Immy said with a bright smile, trying to drum up enthusiasm in the bride.

"Mm-hm. Tomorrow." Those were definitely frown lines on her smooth forehead.

"Is something wrong?" Immy asked.

Loryetta gave a soft sigh, but shook her head. "No, no, nothing's…wrong." She put her smile back on and proceeded around the room.

Soon, most of the guests were seated with heaping plates before them. Hortense filled a plate for herself and joined Immy and Drew. Only some of the women remained in the kitchen or fussed over the buffet table.

Sydney Harbor, the weathered cowboy Immy had met, sat at the next table. His aging cowboy hat rested upside down next to his plate, as the custom was, to preserve the shape of the crown. A purple feather, tucked into the hat band, peeked out. Eccles Justice, the small, tidy man, the father of the bride and the man Sydney had pointed out, passed behind him on his way to a table next to the bride and groom and wedding party. His hat had a big feather in the hat band, too. Immy figured that was the fashion in this town. The men seemed to be trying to outdo each other in the feather department. Mr. Justice bent close to Sydney, but the band quit playing just then and Immy—as well as everyone else—heard his taunt.

"I hope you can remember to use a fork, Syd. You're in civilization now." He noticed the silence and tried to say something else that everyone could hear as another man approached, as large and unkempt as Eccles was small and neat. "Come on, Ned. You remember who Ned Newberry is, Syd?"

Eccles and Ned, who must have been the father of the groom, left Sydney Harbor glowering into his plate as the two mismatched men grinned and shook their heads making their way to the other end of the room.

Immy knew that Ned Newberry had to be the husband of Hortense's cousin, Ouida, and the scoundrel who caused the two women to break off communications a few years ago. Maybe he wasn't in legal trouble anymore, but Immy instantly disliked him, and Eccles too, for their treatment of Sydney Harbor. She wondered what their history was.

Out of the corner of her eye, Immy spied the bride, in her floating veil, with her shoulders hunched, slipping through a door beside the stage at the opposite end of the room from the kitchen.

"Will you watch Drew for a moment?" she asked her mother. "I need to visit the little girls' room." Immy grabbed her purse and followed the bride.

A short hallway beside the stage led to two restrooms, one each for men and women. The thumping and wailing of the band was less distinct with a wall between her and them, but also more annoying. At least there weren't strobe lights in the bathroom.

Immy could see the bride's shoes underneath one of the two metal stall doors. She could also hear her stifled sobs. Just as she'd thought, the bride was upset.

"Loryetta?" She tapped softly on the door. "Can I help you?"

Loryetta opened the door. She'd been sitting on the closed lid, sobbing quietly, the veil still incongruously trailed down her back. Her eye makeup was a mess.

"I don't think anyone can." Her tears flowed freely and she trembled with her distress.

It was sometimes easier to tell your troubles to strangers, Immy thought, so she held out her arms and hugged the woman when she stepped into Immy's embrace, making sure those smudged eyes hadn't stained her blue sweater.

"It's Neddie. I didn't know."

"You don't know what? He's your groom, right? Is he upset about something?"

"Is *he* upset? Why should *he* be upset? It's *me* he's keeping secrets from."

Immy was glad she hadn't asked if "Neddie" was bothered by the music and the lights which, thinking about it, Loryetta's parents might have arranged.

"I just found out." Loryetta pulled away to talk to Immy. "He and his stupid friend have been getting in bar fights. I knew that, but just figured it was guys letting off steam. But now, I come to find out Neddie knifed a guy two months ago in Hillstown."

That didn't sound good. Actually, getting in bar fights didn't sound all that good to Immy to begin with. She pulled a paper towel out of the dispenser and gave it to the distraught bride-to-be.

"And the poor guy is still in the hospital! Neddie could go to jail if he dies."

Was Loryetta upset that Ned Junior was so violent, or that he might go to prison?

"I honestly didn't know he was like that. I mean, I know about the thing in high school. But that was just a one-time thing, I thought."

Immy had to ask. "What was the thing in high school?"

"Oh, Neddie and two other guys from the football team beat up two nerds back then. One had his brain injured and he died. The other one is okay, though. He's in a wheelchair, but he's fine. I'm gonna have to think long and hard about marrying him in the morning."

Immy took a step back. She'd been feeling pretty sorry for the bride, but now she wasn't so sure. She condoned killing and maiming? Being in a wheelchair wasn't fine. "What happened to Ned Junior and his friends from the high school attack?"

Loryetta dabbed at her blackened eyes. "It wasn't exactly an attack. More of just a fight. Nobody official ever found out who did it, and the two boys couldn't tell anyone."

So the one in the wheelchair who was just fine couldn't communicate? Immy took another step back. "Excuse me, I have to use the facilities." She shut herself away in the stall and was happy to hear Loryetta leave the bathroom, after running the water to, presumably, repair her face. Immy managed not to throw up, but just barely. This monstrous prospective groom was the son of Hortense's cousin. Maybe her mother shouldn't have made up with this branch of the family.

Five

As Immy returned to the room, she heard Eccles Justice, the father of the bride, clinking a spoon on a glass, standing by his seat at the head table. Everyone could hear him because the band had just quit playing. The strobe lights had even stopped and the room was now well-lit with glaring overhead lights. Everyone would be able to see their food. She stood where she was to listen to the announcement, wondering why the best man wasn't giving the first toast.

Mr. Justice smiled around at the room as chatter stopped and the people fell silent. "I want y'all to be the very first to know. Ned, stand up and tell the people."

The groom's father stood with an even bigger grin on his broad, weathered face. He towered over the smaller man and managed to look unkempt in almost the exact same sport coat and jeans outfit that Eccles wore so neatly and tidily.

"I'll tell you what. We brought in a gusher today to beat all gushers. Right down there on the new land. Loryetta," he said, raising his beer can in her direction, "your man is gonna be able to support you in style."

Immy found Drew and her mother at their table, which was now fully occupied with other guests.

After Immy sat, Hortense whispered to Immy, "I don't think he would have had a problem with supporting her prior to the discovery of new petroleum reserves." Hortense pointed to her own ring finger on her right hand and shot a pointed look at Ned Newberry.

Immy looked at the large hand Ned held his beer can with. A huge onyx ring flashed in the light.

"See all those diamonds?" Hortense added.

Sure enough, they were close enough to see that the onyx lay surrounded by ring of rather large diamonds.

"How is your cousin?" Immy whispered to her mother, not wanting to discuss the crass subject of money, and the ostentatious announcement, out loud.

"She seems to be getting along satisfactorily. There is something very different about her, but I expect there would be. I knew her before she married that felonious man, Ned Newberry. Tonight, however, the mood is festive and I would say she is pleased about the upcoming marriage and looking forward to uniting the two families in more ways than in business dealings."

Immy was going to ask her more, but Sydney Harbor, who was still sitting at the table next to Immy and her family, stood, knocking his chair over. He threw his napkin onto his plate, grabbed his hat, spat in the direction of Ned and Eccles, and clomped out of the room. As he passed behind Immy on his way out, she heard him muttering over and over, "That's my goddam land. My goddam land, goddammit."

Immy noticed a nice-looking young man who was in the seat next to the one Mr. Harbor had just left. His complexion was light and, even though he kept his head low, nearly in his plate, Immy could see that his face was bright red. The tips of his ears glowed beside his blond hair, cut short. Was he the son of the offended man, Sydney Harbor? It would appear so.

Some of the guests seemed stunned by Sydney's sudden departure, others were amused. But they started to clap for the announcement before he was out the door. Immy and Hortense gave half-hearted soft applause, not thrilled with the way things were going. Hortense even muttered, "How gauche," to express her displeasure at the ostentatious celebration of one's wealth.

The woman sitting across from them had her back to the head table. She rolled her eyes and shook her head slightly as she, too, gave weak applause. Immy was glad to see that some of the others in the room agreed with her mother—and with her. She didn't see how announcing that a wealthy man had just gotten wealthier was appropriate for a wedding rehearsal dinner.

"Wyatt, come on up here." Mr. Justice, the bride's father, beckoned to the red-faced, blushing man Sydney Harbor had left behind.

He turned out to be the best man. He stood beside Mr. Justice and attempted to give a speech. There were apparently some in-jokes that half the room laughed at, things about high school pranks. Nothing as bad as what Loryetta had told Immy, but some of them sounded mean. Actually, most of them sounded mean, if not illegal. The anecdote about how the "ugly" cheerleader ended up made some people laugh. Immy hoped the implication wasn't that she got pregnant. Wyatt didn't speak very long and others lined up to give congratulations and good wishes to the couple.

The woman sitting across the table leaned toward Immy, smiling. "Hi, I'm Lulu Henry. This is my husband, Victor." If Lulu had disapproved of the oil well announcement, which she had seemed to, Victor was still angered by it. His lips were still snarled.

Immy and Hortense introduced themselves and Drew.

"Where are you from?" Lulu asked. "Do you have a place to stay?"

"We're from Saltlick, up by Wymee Falls," Immy said.

"We are registered at the retail hostel at the perimeter of Slap Out," Hortense added.

"It's the Motel Four," Immy quickly added, at Lulu's puzzled look.

"Oh my, is it…is it all right?" Lulu looked worried. "Are you okay there?"

"You don't want to stay there," her husband Victor said. "You'll get bedbugs."

A look passed between the couple, then Lulu spoke. "You come stay with us. We have plenty of room. You can't stay there."

Now a look passed between Hortense and Immy. Hortense gave a mild, insincere protest. "Oh, we couldn't possibly intrude. It's such short notice—"

"Of course, you'll stay with us," Victor said, with finality. His demeanor had softened, gradually, from the stern face he'd made at the oil well announcement.

"I'll bet little Drew will love our dogs." Lulu dug some photos out of her purse and handed them across the table to Drew.

Immy leaned over and looked at them, too. There were three or four, a mixture of breeds.

"Those are nice dogs," Drew said. "I have a pig."

Victor smiled at Immy's daughter. "Do you? That's wonderful." His rather grouchy expression had been completely transformed by talking to Drew. "And guess what we have in our backyard?"

"A pig!" Drew declared confidently.

"No, but almost as good. A little goat."

Drew looked at her mommy, puzzling this out. "Is a goat as good as a pig?"

Immy nodded. "They can be. They're a lot of fun."

"Would you care for more wine? More water?"

Immy looked up at the man standing at her elbow. Her gaze stuck there for a moment, resting on his dark eyes, his perfectly chiseled face, strong jaw, the white teeth and the soft lips that formed his smile.

"Um, yes please."

"Water or wine?"

Immy cleared her throat, finding herself suddenly hoarse. "Yes, please. Um, both. Is that okay?" She wanted to keep him here as long as possible.

His smile deepened and he looked even more attractive, if that was possible. Immy decided she should smile back. She also batted her eyelashes. She couldn't help it.

"Hi, I'm Immy."

With that gorgeous smile, he answered. "Long."

That didn't sound like a name, but he had spoken again. His low, sexy voice matched all the other parts of him. After he filled her glasses, she couldn't help watching him depart either. His back looked as good as his front.

They all sat and toyed with dessert, a mixed berry cobbler that was delicious, while listening to several more speeches. None of the other speeches drew startled reactions, luckily. Just kidding about the couple, mostly about the groom. There was no overt mention of the violence Immy had learned of in the restroom, but other anecdotes of rough and tumble mischief were related.

Eventually, the groom gathered up two other young men. One was the guy who had been helping to cater the dinner, the living embodiment of Adonis. The other was the blushing guy who had been sitting beside Sydney Harbor. She wanted to know more about the one who had been serving, going around to the tables with more water and drinks. It would be a cliché to say he was tall, dark, and handsome, but that's exactly what he was. A strong face and a body with muscles in all the right places. Immy mentally slapped herself for her thoughts. She was living with Ralph, she told herself.

"Long, Wyatt, let's go," Ned Junior slurred. He had been drinking a lot of toasts. The other two were way behind, as far as alcohol consumption went, but Immy thought they might soon catch up. She hoped there would be a designated driver.

"The bachelor party," said Victor. "It's at Skye's The Limit, right up the street."

"Oh, Victor, everything's right up the street in Slap Out," Lulu said, laughing at her husband.

Immy had to agree. There wasn't much to the town. "Is it called that because you can drink as much as you want?"

Lulu laughed again. "No, but it might as well be. The owner is Skye Maxx."

It was settled that they would carefully look their things over for cockroaches and other vermin, then bunk in with the Henrys. Immy took on the duty of saying goodbye to the bride and Hortense made her way to the bride's father, Mr. Justice, to thank him for the dinner. She also wanted to say goodnight to her cousin, Ouida, whom she said she had barely seen, although Immy thought they had talked quite a bit. Drew tagged along after her geemaw, yawning from being up past her usual bedtime.

"We'll see you tomorrow," Immy said, noticing that Loryetta's eyes were still a bit red-rimmed.

Loryetta shook her head slightly. She leaned close and spoke softly. "I don't know. I just don't know." She looked at Immy with her large, sad eyes. "If the guy that Neddie knifed does end up dying, he'll have to go to prison. I don't want to be married to a convict."

Again, Immy concealed her shock that the woman wouldn't mind marrying a murderer, or so it seemed. She just didn't want to marry one who was convicted.

"I don't think I'll sleep a bit tonight," Loryetta mumbled. "I have a decision to make. A big one."

There had been young women at Loryetta's table, presumably the bridesmaids, so Immy hoped they would help the bride out with what would be an easy decision for Immy—dump the guy—but what seemed hard for Loryetta.

"Oh look, Long left his bungees here," Loryetta said. She picked up one of the stretchy cords from the small pile on the shelf in the opening into the kitchen. A tag hung from it that read "Long Catering." So Long must actually be the name of the Greek god, Immy thought. She was having a hard time thinking of "long" as a person's name. "He ties down the big plastic tubs in his truck with these," Loryetta explained.

Immy didn't want to seem overly curious about the good-looking Long, so she didn't ask any questions.

The three drove through town to just outside it on the other side, where the Henrys lived. On the way, they passed Skye's The Limit. It wasn't bad looking. There was a big window in the front that was clean enough to clearly see the three guys at the bar, Ned Newberry, Jr., and his two friends, raising mugs of suds and slopping them all over themselves. Closer to the window, in a seat next to it, was Sydney Harbor, slumped against the glass and watching them with a morose expression on his face.

A pickup in front of the place had "Long Catering" lettered on the door. Loryetta had called him that, so Long was definitely at least part of his name.

Eccles Justice and Ned Newberry, the fathers of the "happy" couple, walked up to the front door and entered it as Immy slowed to take in the scene. She couldn't very well park in the middle of the street to stay and spy, and there were no empty parking spots. In fact, it looked like Eccles and Ned had walked over from the church. She was curious about what would happen when all of these drunk, rather volatile men were together without the women, but drove on. She was sure she would find out in the morning.

The Henrys' house was easy to find with Lulu's directions, a little way beyond the edge of town. A pickup and a small SUV were in the driveway, but there was plenty of room for the van.

Lulu Henry opened the door before they got to it and ushered them in as Victor came out and took the luggage. Lulu was proud of her 1950s house. She told them it was only two years old, but they'd had it constructed to look like a movie set for a fifties film. There was painted wainscoting, lots of aqua and pink, and even a vintage-looking refrigerator with a rounded top. Immy began to understand the theme more deeply when Lulu introduced the dogs to them.

"This one is Lucy," she said as a cute corgi waddled up to Immy. A pug followed, wagging his stump. "That's Ricky. The basset hound is Ethel, and Phreddie is Ricky's litter mate. We had to spell it Phreddie," she spelled it out, "since she's a girl and we needed the name Fred."

When Immy asked about that, Lulu readily admitted *The Lucy Show* was the theme of their life. Immy wondered what Victor thought about this, but he smiled with delight as Lulu led them through the house pointing out all the fifties details. He was totally on board, obviously.

"Where's your goat?" Drew asked, stuffing her fist in her mouth to mask a big yawn.

"It's too dark to see him now," Victor told her. "You can meet Babalu in the morning." Immy had to stifle a giggle. Lulu noticed and Immy smiled at her. "Your pets' names are…perfect. Just perfect." She knew that name, Babalu, must have some sort of association with Desi and Lucy.

"It would be propitious to get Nancy Drew to a place where she can slumber, soon," Hortense said, noting Drew's nonstop yawning and droopy eyelids.

"Oh my yes, you must be tired, after the drive and everything." Lulu led the way to a charming guest bedroom with twin beds. It was straight from the TV setting. Immy hardly noticed the furnishings, though. She quickly washed up, let Drew skip brushing her teeth, and fell into one of the beds with Drew, exhausted. Not even her mother's snoring in the other twin bed, which started approximately 120 seconds after her head touched down on the pillow, could keep her awake.

*****

Immy sat up, wide awake, wondering where she was. Oh yes, the Lucy House in Slap Out. She realized that the reason she had woken up was that her bladder was telling her to do something about the wine she'd had at the rehearsal dinner. After she quietly used the bathroom, she saw a light on somewhere else in the house. She crept out of the bedroom to find Lulu and Victor at the kitchen table. Lulu reached over to pat her husband's shoulder as Immy came into the room.

"There's nothing anyone can do," Victor said, taking hold of Lulu's hand. He nodded at Immy as he rose. "Night."

After he left the room, Lulu remained, not looking happy.

"Is everything all right? Is there anything I can do?"

"What Victor said is true. No one can do anything. Ned Newberry used to be a crooked car dealer and now he's a crooked real estate dealer."

"He went to prison for the car thing, right?" Immy had heard Hortense talk about her cousin's husband and used the term "horse thief" often. Hortense equated horses to cars, as they were both transportation.

"Yes." Lulu shook her head. "Now he's up to new tricks."

"What did Mr. Harbor mean about the oil well being on his land?"

"Exactly what he said. Sydney retired to do some ranching, just a small herd, with his son, Wyatt, after his wife died. He bought a parcel of land from Ned, not too many acres, but enough to run some cattle. He spent a couple of years planting good grass and getting a herd started. Then Ned drilled a few feet onto his land and hit oil. Lots of it. Sydney has tried for several years in the courts to get his oil rights back, but Ned has a document signed by Sydney that says he only bought surface rights. The court thought Sydney should know that he had to buy the mineral rights, but he didn't."

"So Ned can just drill on his land?"

"Not all over, but he can drill on part of it."

"And Mr. Harbor didn't know about that?"

"Not every Texan knows everything. A lot of us didn't know about those rights being separate."

"I guess we should get to sleep for the wedding tomorrow," Immy said, wanting to cut this unpleasant discussion off, while wondering if there would really be a wedding.

"I guess we should. I'm going early to help in the kitchen for the dinner afterward. I hope you sleep well."

Lulu gave her a smile, so Immy thought she was in an okay mood now. She hoped so.

Six

IT WAS A HUSTLE AND A BUSTLE AND A HALF, getting everyone ready for the wedding in the Henrys' smallish house. There weren't quite enough bathrooms for five people at once, but the guest room did have its own, so Immy, Hortense, and Drew all managed to eat a hurried breakfast of cereal, juice, and coffee supplied by Lulu, and head for the church in plenty of time. The Henrys had left well before Immy's family, since Immy was having a time getting Drew into the new, stiff dress they had brought for her. When the three were arrayed in their finery, Drew in the puffy dress, Immy in a decent pair of actual slacks and a blouse and Hortense in a loose, flowing purple concoction, they finally set out.

As soon as she entered the sanctuary Immy spotted Lulu sitting a few rows in front of them. Her business in the kitchen must be done, Immy thought. Victor came in quite a bit later, but no one was actually late. In fact, they were still sitting on the hard pews a good half hour after the time the wedding was to begin. The sanctuary was packed. Everyone was there but the wedding party. When she stretched around and looked behind her, Immy could see what looked like bridesmaids and groomsmen milling about in the vestibule, passing by the sanctuary entrance, back and forth.

Lulu and Victor got up and walked past Immy and her family.

"Where are you going?" Immy asked.

Lulu leaned over and whispered. "Victor forgot to leave water out for the goat."

They continued up the aisle and out of the church while Immy and her mother gave each other a look.

"What was that about?" Immy whispered to her mother. Although she could have used a normal voice since the room was getting noisier because everyone had been there so long that they were starting to chatter.

Hortense answered, not in a whisper. "Perhaps they just want to exit and not witness the nuptials. They don't seem to like either of the families involved, the bride's or the groom's."

A buzz eventually began to fill the room as the people moved from whispering to talking aloud, wondering what the holdup was. Another long period of time went by. Something had to be happening.

"Do you suppose he's jilted her?" Immy said, leaning close to Hortense so others wouldn't hear her damning query. She wondered, not out loud, if Loryetta had called it off.

"It is more probable that the groom is suffering from the aftereffects of the overabundance of alcohol he most likely imbibed late yesterday evening."

Immy wondered if a hangover would keep the groom from showing up, though. Surely many grooms got married with a hangover from their bachelor party.

Heads turned when a disheveled man in an expensive suit stumbled up the aisle. It was Ned Newberry, father of the groom. His hair, normally slightly mussed, was unkempt, his jacket unbuttoned, and his once-shiny shoes tracked mud on the carpeting.

"He's gone," Ned sobbed. "My boy's gone." He staggered and stood in the aisle, grasping the back of a pew.

Before Immy could finish forming the thought that Ned Junior, the groom, had indeed, jilted poor Loryetta, Ned continued, dropping to his knees and wailing at the ceiling of the sanctuary. "I found him. They've killed him! Killed him dead!"

Oh no! That was much worse than abandoning the bride. Several men jumped up from the pews and rushed to Ned. Two of them pulled him to his feet. Some people shifted to make room and the men sat him at the end of the nearest pew.

Mrs. Ouida Newberry was still seated in the first row, sitting stiffly, staring straight ahead.

"Excuse me." Hortense rose and ran, actually ran, down the aisle to her cousin Ouida.

"Where's Geemaw going?" asked Drew.

"She wants to talk to her cousin. That's her son they're talking about, that just died."

A wall of dark-suited men surrounded Ned, but only for a few moments. A man wearing a police uniform soon strode in, then Ned was led out of the sanctuary.

Hortense returned. "I think the poor woman is partially catatonic. Some of the townspeople are going to take care of her, poor thing."

Immy's next thought was for Loryetta, probably because she had talked to her the night before.

"Maybe you could take Drew out of here."

"Yes, I concur. This is not the ideal atmosphere for a young child."

Immy watched her mother and daughter leave the sanctuary and went to find the bride.

The vestibule was now crowded, not only with the bridesmaids and groomsmen, but with others who had rushed out, following Ned and the officer. Immy saw Ned being driven away in a Slap Out police car. The bride wasn't anywhere to be seen. Immy stopped for a moment to hear what was being said.

"Crane had better call in someone from Mammoth. He can't handle something like this."

"Maybe the state troopers should be called."

"Tied to the walkin' beam, can you believe that?"

"Pumpjack just pumpin' away with Junior tied up on there."

She tried to make sense of what they were saying as she hurried to find a restroom. That was probably where the bride was, she figured, since that's where she'd gone when she was upset before.

The restrooms weren't too easy to find in this large, rambling church building, and there were a lot of them, unlike in the annex from last night, but Immy dashed around and checked them all. She didn't find Loryetta. Maybe she had already left. There was no reason for her to be here now, after all. Immy wondered how she felt, not wanting to marry Ned Junior, then having her Neddie turn up dead. If he was, indeed, dead, and tied to the crossbar on the oil well pump, someone had to have put him there.

After her wanderings up and down the hallways, checking out every restroom she could find, she headed back toward the center of the church. The front double doors stood wide open, meant to welcome the town folk to a joyous celebration. People were starting to drift out, making their way down the grand concrete stairway and to the parking lot at the side. The Henrys were bucking traffic and coming in, up the stairs and through the doors. They must have left at some point and were coming back.

"Lulu, Victor," Immy said. "Do you know what happened?"

"Is the sheriff here?" Lulu asked. "We have to talk to him."

"He just left. He had Ned Newberry in the car with him."

Lulu and Victor passed a private look between them.

"Is his son really dead? Murdered?"

Lulu took a breath. "We found him."

"Well, Phreddie found him," Victor said.

Lulu nodded. "He set up such a racket. I've never heard him howl like that."

"We ran out to see what was wrong with him."

"There's a pump jack a little ways behind our house."

Immy had noticed that they did have some oil wells close to their place. There were others right inside in the town. That might be strange to think about, but she knew other small towns had them right on the main streets, next to houses.

Lulu continued. "We saw him right away. There he was. Tied to the thing, bobbing up and down."

"Didn't hurt the pump at all," Victor added. "It just kept stroking."

"So you called the sheriff?" Immy asked.

"We called Ned, too," Lulu said. "We thought him and Ouida oughta know. We hung around for a while. Chief Crane was tryin' to figure out what to do."

"Who to call," Victor said.

"Then Ned jumped in his car and took off."

"So the sheriff went after him."

"He came here," Immy said. "Maybe he wanted people here to know. Do you know where Loryetta is?"

They shook their heads in unison. "I suppose she came here," Lulu said. "Unless she didn't."

Immy couldn't argue with that logic.

Victor held out a key. "If you want to go back to our place, just let yourselves in. I think we'll stick around here for a while and see what happens."

Immy kind of wanted to stick around too, but nothing was going to happen at the church. Maybe they should go back to the Henrys' and see what the scene of the crime looked like. Her PI senses were tingling. She found Hortense and Drew in a little chapel where it was quiet.

"I believe we should vacate these premises and find seating that is more comfortable."

The pews there were the same wooden ones as those in the sanctuary.

"Those benches are really, really hard." Drew rubbed her bottom.

"Nancy Drew, dear, do not touch that part of your anatomy in public."

"Well, they are."

"Yes, I am constrained to agree with you. They are called pews."

"Do they stink?"

"I suppose they do at times." Hortense turned to Immy. "Imogene, shall we endeavor to locate a place that serves comestibles?"

Being hungry was a good sign that her mother wasn't terribly upset. "Let's do that." Immy led the way to their van.

Seven

THERE WASN'T A WIDE CHOICE OF EATING ESTABLISHMENTS of eating establishments in Slap Out, but the one they found had perfectly acceptable food, both for Hortense and for Drew, which was a feat. Not every diner could satisfy both of them. It sat perched at the side of the main highway through town going east and west. As opposed to the main highway through town going north and south. All of the other roads were narrow and full of potholes and could barely be called roads, but these two were paved. Immy thought the state probably took care of the two good ones. They seemed to be state routes.

They entered the small building to a steamy atmosphere that smelled delicious. Onions and garlic and fried food. Immy felt herself getting more and more hungry as they took seats and looked over the thin menus.

Hortense ordered liver and onions, one of her favorite meals. Drew got a grilled cheese sandwich, and Immy settled for a burger and fries. The iced tea was excellent. Immy thought they probably cleaned out the big metal brewer pretty often, since it didn't have that rancid taste that the iced tea sometimes had. She had noticed that tang in Wymee Falls restaurants.

Immy wolfed down her meal, sharing some french fries with Drew, then jiggled her knee up and down, impatient to get out to the Henrys' place and check out the pumpjack. Ned Junior wouldn't still be on it, most likely. But what if he was? What if there were clues she could discover? She didn't have her full certification yet to be an official private eye, but she was confident that she would soon, and a solved crime under her belt would be a real feather in her cap. If something under a belt could lead to a feather in a cap.

Hortense finished soon after Immy, but wanted a dessert menu.

"Can we get something to go?" Immy asked. "Maybe some cookies?"

Her mother admitted that would be acceptable.

"Drew, can we take the rest of that with us?" Maybe they would soon be back out at the house. She only had a fourth of the grilled cheese left on her sturdy china plate.

Drew insisted on finishing her "sammich" and, for once, chewed and swallowed each bite, one by one. Immy gritted her teeth and felt her fingers curling. Of course she couldn't urge her daughter to bolt her food when, up until this point in her young life, Immy had been trying to get her to slow down and eat exactly as she was now doing.

There was nothing to do but wait. Immy made a conscious decision to follow some relaxation tips she had read online. She lowered her shoulders. They were surprisingly tense and high. Then she peeled her tongue from off the roof of her mouth. Strange how that tongue got up there all the time. Then she loosened her jaw. Yep, it was tight.

How wonderful that Drew finished as soon as Immy had completed the ritual. She hurried to pay, collecting the cookies at the counter as they left.

The drive to the Henrys' place was flat and uneventful, until they were almost there. Then they were met with two sheriff cars, an ambulance, and a fire truck leaving the property, and all flashing their lights. Although none were using sirens. There was no urgency involved with transporting a dead body, after all.

"Did they have a fire here?" Drew asked, her eyes wide at the vehicles driving past them.

"No, dear," Hortense answered. "There was a man who was sick and they came to tend him."

That was quick thinking. Immy silently congratulated her mother for avoiding upsetting Drew.

"Is he all better now?"

Immy noticed her mother hesitating. She didn't like to lie to her granddaughter, but Immy knew she didn't want to discuss a dead guy and a murder in front of her either. So she jumped in.

"Yes, Drew, he's just fine now." Would Drew find out her mother had lied and would she be upset about it? Immy had to figure out how to tell her more, without telling her all of it. She would do that later.

For now, she wanted Drew and Hortense to go inside the Henrys' cute little 1950s house so she could wander around outside and find the scene of the crime. She had to do it before Lulu and Victor got home in case they thought it was a bad idea. She wondered where they were, but maybe they had gone out to eat, too. She thought she knew how she could handle this.

"Drew, I think it's time for your bath." Drew always loved her bath and Immy had made sure to bring along some rubber duckies. "Mother, could you help her to do that?"

"I most assuredly can do that, Imogene. Nancy Drew, let us collect your bath accoutrements." Did her mother give her a wink? Did she know what her daughter was hankering to do?

"These dogs should probably go out," Immy said. They looked perfectly satisfied where they were, lying on the living room rug, but they seemed to know the words "go" and "out." The pug jumped up first, then the other three followed, heading for the back door at varying speeds, depending on the lengths of their legs. Although none of them had very long legs, so top speed was not lightning fast.

Immy was surprised when her mother gave her another covert wink. She had figured out Immy's plan, for sure.

When the back door was opened, two of the dogs ran to the fence at the back of the yard, leaving the other two to leisurely scout locations nearer the house. Immy followed the runners. She had brought a leash for only one, so she chose Phreddie, clipped the leash onto his, or rather

her, collar, and they went out through the back gate. Lucy, the Corgi, seemed a bit miffed, but got over it soon.

Immy spied what must be the goat, in the corner of the yard, but it didn't approach them.

It started sprinkling slightly. Immy gave the clouds a dirty look. "Don't you dare pour on me right now."

The basset hound put her nose down and went straight to the oil field a little ways behind the house. The rain came down a little harder and she wished she had an umbrella with her. She also wished the ground wasn't mostly dirt. The wind shifted and blew the sulfur smell from the oil well toward her. She waved it away with her free hand. How could the dog smell anything else out here? Wouldn't that awful stench cover everything else up? But Phreddie selected one of the pumps nearby and sniffed the ground excitedly.

"So this is the one, huh? This is where he was?" The awful smell was strong here. Immy would look around quickly, then leave as soon as she could. She didn't want to go back into the house with this odor on her clothes, and in her damp hair.

There was no evidence left that this had been a crime scene. No yellow tape, no police on duty, guarding the clues. Maybe there weren't any. Immy gazed up at the arm of the pump, going up and down with lazy precision, pumping that oil out of the ground, into a tank at the edge of the field. The counterweight was equally dependable, making rhythmic circles, driving the arm up and down. Over and over. Clanking and groaning. Day after day, looking like a giant grasshopper, stuck in place. How had they gotten his body down, Immy wondered? She didn't think anyone ever stopped the pumping. For that matter, how did the killer get the body up there? The arm had to be moving while he did that. Was there more than one person? She thought there would have to be. One man, even a strong one, couldn't climb this thing carrying deadweight.

The rain stopped suddenly. Dusk was falling and it was getting hard to see, but Immy strained to look for footprints. That was hopeless, she soon decided. The place was full of them. Everyone in those multiple vehicles that had just left had trampled all over this ground. It was bare ground, with a bit of ivy in places, and would have held a solitary print nicely, but this was just a muddled mess now. The shower hadn't helped anything.

Phreddie gave a little yip and waggled his rear end. *Her* rear end. Immy had a hard time thinking of a dog named, essentially, Freddie, as being a girl dog. Immy bent down to see what she was excited about. Phreddie gave a big huff and something flew up. It was a feather, or a piece of a feather, a broken part of a feather. It floated upward on an invisible draft of air for a moment, then drifted down and landed next to a clump of what looked like poison ivy. Immy picked it up, avoiding the ivy. The feather was dark blue, or maybe purple, or maybe gray or black. The sun had set and it was getting dark. There was also a lot of mud on it and it was really only half a feather, or less.

Was this the feather Sydney Harbor had worn last night? It wasn't really purple now, if it ever had been. The feather in Eccles Justice's hat had been dark, too. Maybe it was popular to wear a dark color. Maybe many people even wore purple.

Immy closed her eyes and pictured the scuffle as someone killed Ned Junior, then had to get him onto that crossbeam. Did the killer's hat get knocked off? Did this feather fall out of the band, get stepped on and broken? If so, she realized she probably shouldn't be touching it with her bare hands. If this was evidence, it should go into an evidence bag. Oh well, she had already picked it up, and she didn't have any evidence bags handy. She stuck it into her bra. She would save it and show it to the authorities later.

Her phone rang and she fished it out of her jacket pocket.

"Immy? Can you talk?"

She was surprised to hear the bride's voice. Loryetta was crying, it sounded like. "Yes, I sure can. I'm so sorry for all of this. Are you going to be okay?"

"No, I'll never be okay again. They've just arrested my daaad!" She wailed on this last word.

"Arrested your dad? They really did?" They couldn't have solved this crime already, could they? "Did they cuff him and read him his rights?" She had learned a lot in her PI course. And from the extensive reading she had done in that valuable book, *The Moron's Compleat PI Guidebook*, from the Moron's Compleat Guidebook series.

"Well, not exactly. They said they needed to take him in for questioning. Is that different?"

"It's not exactly the same thing. No, it seems he's not arrested officially. But…I don't understand. You were getting married to Neddie." She would have been if she had decided not to back out. The last thing Immy knew, she had been wavering. "Why would your dad kill him? Your new husband?"

"Where are you? I have to talk to someone in person. I can't talk about this on the phone."

Immy certainly didn't know her well, but she thought maybe the woman wanted to talk to someone who wasn't from around here. That made sense. The locals had maybe made up their minds. Maybe they had all decided Loryetta's dad, Eccles Justice, had killed Ned Newberry, Jr.

She and Loryetta agreed to meet at the cemetery at the edge of town. Loryetta told Immy how to get there and Immy urged Phreddie to finish doing her business, then tugged her back inside the fence. She ran into the house, past the animals, and poked her head inside the steamy, fragrant bathroom, where Drew was holding court with bubbles and her duckies while Hortense perched on the closed toilet seat trying to swipe a washcloth over the back of Drew's neck, grunting as she leaned over the edge of the tub.

"I have to go somewhere for a few minutes," Immy said and closed the door before either of them could ask any questions.

After she towel dried her hair and gave it a brushing, she drove to the cemetery trying to remember exactly what the feather in Eccles Justice's cowboy hat had looked like at the rehearsal dinner. Too many of the local men wore hats with feathers.

Eight

WITH LORYETTA'S DIRECTIONS, THE CEMETERY WASN'T HARD TO FIND. She had told Immy to follow the main road west out of town. The clouds were still thick, so she turned on the headlights in the van. And there it was, caught in her headlights, a nice big expanse of mostly dead grass, at this time of year, which was studded, of course, with marble headstones. Immy pulled up onto the narrow gravel drive and took the van through the rather grand gate, consisting of two brick pillars with wing walls, fronted by a couple of small crepe myrtles still blooming, and all sitting under the overarching metal sign declaring that this was, indeed, the "Slap Out Cemetery."

The thickening clouds plunged the cemetery deeper into gloom and darkness. As she wended her way down the row, the headstones cast eerie shadows that moved as her car lights passed by. It seemed like a place where you could find a ghost. Especially at this time in the late afternoon. She soon spotted the grimy white pickup that belonged to Mr. Justice, Loryetta's father. Immy could tell because the license plate read:

MR JUSTC

The woman sat on the tailgate, dressed now in jeans and a denim jacket, turquoise cowgirl boots on her feet. Immy thought that this was quite a transformation. She looked nothing like the beautiful bride from the reception. Her hair was a mess, caught up in a lump on top of her head, and her face was bare of all the makeup she'd worn last night. Although that makeup had been streaked when Immy saw it in the bathroom. Immy thought it looked like she'd been crying all night. Surely she had gotten ready for the wedding and that would require makeup.

Immy climbed out of the van and perched on the tailgate, beside her. It was only slightly damp. She patted the woman's shoulder tentatively, not sure how to comfort her, being a stranger and all.

"Oh Immy," Loryetta wailed, and threw her arms around Immy. That settled the question of how to comfort her. Immy hugged her in return, rubbing her back softly and murmuring something like, "I'm so so sorry, so sorry," not being sure what she was sorry for, but thinking it was the right thing to say at a moment like this. She knew she shouldn't say, "Everything is gonna be okay," because it wasn't gonna be. She disliked it when people said everything was okay when it wasn't.

Eventually, Loryetta lifted her head and leaned back a bit. "I need somebody to talk to. I can't talk to anybody else."

"You can talk to me. I won't tell anyone what you say." Well, unless she admitted to killing her intended. But this tiny woman couldn't possibly have hauled him onto that crossbeam. Not without help.

"Everything is such a mess. I thought it was gonna work out. I mean, Neddie was reformed. He wasn't ever gonna hurt nobody again. He swore to me on a bible. Everything was fine until Neddie's pa had to blab last night about that new well."

Immy clearly remembered Ned Newberry standing up and announcing that a "gusher" had come in. He had seemed to direct his speech to Sydney Harbor, and Mr. Harbor had stalked out in anger soon after the short speech. Immy had always assumed that hitting black gold with a new oil well was a good thing. A very good thing. Until she talked to Lulu last night.

"Was he not supposed to say anything about it?"

"Well, he had to, sometime or other. But not right there, with Sydney sitting right there. Poor Sydney."

Immy was about to ask what she thought was poor about him when she continued. "That was supposed to be his property, you know. I mean it was his property. It *is* his property."

"So why was he upset about it?"

"He bought it from Daddy and Daddy and Ned never told him he didn't have the rights. The mineral rights. You have to do that separate and they never told him that."

"You mean they drilled a well on his property, and it's a good one, and he can't get any money from the oil?" This jibed with what Lulu had been saying.

Loryetta nodded. "That's exactly right. Daddy and Ned been doing that to people every once in a while, the last few years. Neddie's mama said it was awful for Sydney, and for his son, Wyatt."

Immy remembered that Sydney had left alone. His son had stayed behind, though, and had even gone out with Ned Junior afterwards. "Was Wyatt upset too?"

"I imagine so. Wouldn't you be?"

"I mean, he went out with the other guys, with Ned Junior and the other one, to that bar."

"Long. Long Tuttle. That's the other guy's name. Those are three musketeers. All through school they've always hung out together. We always used to call Long 'Hot Mike,' though, on account of Long doesn't sound like a name."

Immy had to agree. She was right. It was more of an adjective. But Hot Mike didn't sound like a name either. "His name is Long and you call him Mike?"

"Long Michael Tuttle. That's his full name. But he was hot in high school."

Immy clearly remembered which one he was, the one she had wanted to flirt with, and thought he was pretty darn hot now, too. "So, should I call him Long or Mike?"

She shrugged. "When you gonna be talking to him?"

Immy shrugged. "I might see him around." The hot guy had actually been on her mind during the night, ever since she had seen him at the reception. So tall, dark, and handsome. How could she not have him on her mind? "So they're all three good friends?"

"From forever."

"If your dad didn't do anything wrong, he'll be okay. They're just questioning him. Taking his statement. Finding out what he knows about everything that happened last night. They have to do that to eliminate him as a suspect. From the investigation." Immy felt herself throwing around legal words to impress Loryetta.

"Well, he sure didn't kill Neddie. That would be stupid."

As well as criminal, Immy thought. Immoral, sinful, a lot of things way worse than stupid. Again, she wondered how skewed the value system of this woman was.

"How do you know so much stuff about the law?" Loryetta asked. "About statements and investigation and stuff?"

"I'm studying to become a PI."

"What's that? Pee Eye? I thought that was something from math class."

Immy frowned a moment. "Oh, pi. No, it's the letters P and I. It's an abbreviation. It stands for Private Investigator."

"What? Like, a cop?"

"No, not exactly. A person who investigates things for, well, for private people, I guess." Maybe Immy should learn a little more about that title.

"That sounds kinda interesting."

"Oh, it is. I've learned so much about police procedures, and about the law."

"Well, what is it that you do, exactly?"

"I solve crimes. For people who pay me to do that." Ideally.

Loryetta jumped up from the truck bumper, her eyes blinking like a hazard light. "You can find out who killed my Neddie?"

Was she going to offer Immy a job? Could this trip work out to be something very, very good? "I could. If I was hired to do that."

"So, how does it work?"

"Someone has to hire me. We work out my fee, then I find things out for them."

"You charge money for doing it?"

"Well, yes. It's a job."

"Huh. Lemme talk to Daddy, if they'll let me. I'll let you know." She went around to the driver's door.

"Do you want my phone number?" Immy called. Why had she not brought her business cards with her on this trip? After this, she would bring them everywhere. You never knew when there would be a crime to solve. Loryetta came back to the rear of the truck and handed Immy her cell phone. When Immy keyed in her number, she called herself "Imogene D PI."

"Great," Loryetta said, looking at the entry after Immy handed her phone back. "I'll let you know."

"Wait, I need to ask you a couple of questions, I guess. The last time you saw Ned Junior was at the dinner?"

"Yep." She nodded.

"So the other two, Wyatt and Long, would be the last to see him? Besides the killer? Does he live with his parents?"

"No, he has an apartment here in town. There aren't very many of them, but a couple of the big old houses are divided up into apartments."

"So he probably went home after the drinking?"

Loryetta shrugged. "He said he wanted to be good and ready. He was going to maybe sleep in his car and not be late."

"So he would be sleeping in his tux?"

"I'm not sure. I hope not. But maybe. He doesn't always have good sense, I guess. I'll go give Daddy your number now, okay?"

Immy watched her speed away, throwing up some of the sparse gravel on the narrow road. She was swerving a bit, but didn't knock down any tombstones. That was good. This was all good. All but the dead guy.

Nine

IMMY STOOD WATCHING LORYETTA DRIVE AWAY, having second thoughts, right after those first ones. She wondered how on earth she would find the killer. She didn't know this place. She didn't know these people. She didn't know, well, what she was doing.

Did she even want to do this? The more she had learned about Loryetta, the less she thought of her. Did she want to work for a woman who thought putting a guy in a wheelchair was high school hijinks? Who thought that stabbing people was okay as long as you didn't go to prison for it?

Maybe her "Daddy" wouldn't want to cough up the money. She would have to give a lot of thought to the money. Hmm. She would charge them a huge amount. Then they wouldn't hire her.

There was something else she had to do right now, though, while she was alone, with no one around to hear, just in case things got all lovey-dovey. She had to call Ralph. There were half a dozen missed calls from him on her phone. He must have been missing her a lot.

She got back into the van and closed the door. The clouds had thickened and she wondered if a downpour was coming.

"Immy? Where are you? Are you okay?"

"I am, but…"

"Look, I want to talk to you, but I can't right now. We're hot on the trail of a criminal."

Ooo, that sounded so sexy. Probably because it involved the word "hot." And because Ralph was saying it in his deep cop voice.

"What happened? Is it a murder?"

"No, a robbery."

"Wow, a bank heist. In Saltlick?"

He chuckled. She was sure he was laughing with her, not at her. "No, not quite. It's the library."

"Someone robbed the library? They stole the books?"

"No, not the books. Look, I have to go. We need to catch this guy."

With that, he cut off the call, leaving her hanging, wondering what was going on back home. Her mother had worked at that library for many years, but it had never been robbed. As far as Immy knew, it wasn't a favorite place of criminals, although some probably used the computers. She would just have to wait for Ralph to call her back. She couldn't interrupt him when he was hot on the trail.

She needn't have worried about any lovey-dovey happening.

It was back to Slap Out and the problems there. She would be home soon enough. The shadows of those tombstones danced around again on her way out. Were they more animated now? They were more vivid, blacker. It would soon be night.

Slowly, she drove back to the Henrys', wavering from one minute to the next about whether or not she should take this case. If it became a case.

A case? If it did materialize, she'd have to give it a name. That had to be the first step. She didn't have file folders here, which was a big disadvantage, so she would have to imagine the name of the case written on a tab. Now, what to call it? The Case of the…Gutted Groom. But had he been gutted? She had no idea how he had been killed. Probably shot, since these people were all cowboys. They carried guns, not knives. Well, maybe he'd been strangled. They all had ropes. And poor Junior's body had been tied to that crossbeam with a rope, surely.

The Case of the Wrecked Wedding. That did have the right ring to it. It wasn't easy to say out loud, though. The Case of the Grody Groom.

The Groaning Groom, The Gross Groom. Trying a different tactic, she came up with The Pummeling at the Pumpjack, The Pumpjack Passion Affair, The Stroke of Death. WAIT, that one was promising, since the arm of the pump stroked up and down. But it wasn't alliterative. Something would occur to her. A Case had to have a snappy name.

The clouds had blown away without drowning everybody, Immy was glad to note. There was a truck in front of the Henrys' place that didn't belong to them. Had she seen it before? A shiny red truck, kind of small, so probably not a working ranch truck. She spotted the side as she pulled up next to it and saw the sign. Aha, this was Long Tuttle's truck with the Long Catering logo on it. Was that Greek god in this house? Her heart quickened.

She climbed out of the van and entered the front door. No one seemed to be there, not even the dogs. So she went through to the back and found everyone in the yard. Long Hot Mike was there, too, holding a leash. They were all crowded around, so she couldn't see if there was a dog or cat at the end of it until she came closer. Hot Mike waved to her and shot her a sexy grin. "Hey, Immy. Glad you're here. Have you met Babalu?"

He was glad she was here. That didn't help her heart rate. "Babalu?" Had she heard that word somewhere before? Her brain wouldn't work at the moment.

Lulu supplied the answer. "It's the name of a song by Desi Arnaz."

Of course it was. Hortense did sometimes watch reruns of *I Love Lucy* and Immy liked them too. She was confused. Was this the goat she had seen, vaguely, in the dark? "So is this your goat or his?" she asked Lulu. She couldn't see Hot Mike naming a goat that.

"We've been keeping him while we decide," Lulu said. "We're considering some of the factors."

"We're renting until we make up our minds," Victor added.

"You can rent baby goats?" Immy looked at the tiny thing. It looked like a baby.

The small goat greeted her with something that sounded like "Maa" or maybe "Meh." Immy drew back, startled by the eyes on the little creature. The pupils weren't right. Instead of pupils, there were horizontal strips. "Are his eyes okay?"

Hot Mike answered both her questions in words, again with that fabulous smile. His teeth were so white and even. "I have a side business renting them out to trim grass and stuff. They love to eat poison ivy. This one's a miniature, though, not a baby. He won't ever be able to get through much grass. I got him as a pet, but the other goats bully him, so he has to have a new home. And yes, they have unusual eyes."

Immy took another look. The little goat was gazing at her with those sideways rectangle pupils. If Lulu had already named him with an *I Love Lucy* name, her money would be on Lulu and Victor keeping him.

"He's awfully cute." He was, aside from his spooky eyes. Immy leaned down to touch the soft hair on his back. The inquisitive little guy twisted around and licked her hand. She was smitten. He gave out a louder sound. A bleat, she would call it.

"Mommy, mommy, mommy." Drew tugged on Immy's arm, the one not petting the goat. "Can we get one, too? Please please please?"

"Now, Nancy Drew, one must cogitate for a period of time before making a commitment such as this." Hortense was, however, gazing at the little guy with what looked to Immy like adoration.

Immy's phone chirped and she drew it out to glance at the number. It was Ralph. Calling back already? She would make him wait, since he'd been so rude to her. When she put it back into her pocket Hortense shot her a look. Had she muttered his name? She knew her mother wanted her to make up with Ralph. To at least accept his calls. Should she tell her mother the library had been robbed? Maybe she didn't have enough details yet to tell her. There might be a big reaction, overreaction more likely, when Hortense learned that her beloved library had been violated.

"I'll call him back later," she said to everyone, but for Hortense's benefit.

She was thirsty from talking and from the drive to and from the cemetery, so she left them outside and went into the kitchen for something to drink. A big pitcher of sun tea was sitting on the counter. She felt the belly of the rounded pitcher and it was still warm. Lulu must have brewed it outside today. Would she be able to leave sun tea in the backyard in the future, with a goat there? Okay, *if* a goat were there?

For now, Immy foraged for a glass in the cupboard, popped in a lot of ice, and poured the liquid goodness over the cubes. It was made nice and strong, so the melting ice cubes made it drinkable, not weak.

She was about to rejoin everyone in the yard when they started coming back in. Lulu and Long sat at the kitchen table where she wrote out a check and signed a contract for him.

"Thanks, Miss Lulu." He folded the check into his copy of the contract and slipped them into his jacket pocket as he rose. He gave a slight head nod to Immy when he passed her. It seemed significant, so she followed him to the living room.

"Wanna go out and grab something?" he asked, turning on that smile.

"I think so." She answered him with a smile that she hoped he found just as appealing. "When you thinking of? I have a couple of things to do. Won't take long." She wanted to write out everything she knew about her new Case before details evaporated. She needed a list of who to question, what questions to ask them, clues if there were any besides her feather. Oh, she needed to put that somewhere, too. It was still tickling her inside her bra.

"Meet me at the diner in half an hour?"

"Perfect." She stood watching him go for a few seconds, admiring the rear parts of the man. Of course, thoughts of Ralph immediately assailed her and she experienced a wave of guilt. It left soon, though.

Victor and Drew had remained in the yard with Babalu. Immy wondered if she'd ever get Drew inside the house again. She could hear the cute sounds of the goat and the equally cute squeals of her daughter, trying to mimic him.

"Imogene." Hortense came up behind her. "Would you mind

supervising your offspring with that miniature bovid?"

Did she not trust Victor to do that? Probably not. "Mother, I can't right now. I have something to do."

"Something that takes precedence over your daughter's safety and well-being in the company of a hooved animal that has sharp keratin growths protruding from its cranium?"

"It's tiny, Mother. And I have a Case." Oops. She hadn't intended to say that.

"Is that true?" Her mother narrowed her eyes. She obviously suspected her daughter was lying.

Why couldn't her mother understand how important it was for her to have a Case? She had to be honest. "Well, I'm not sure yet. But I might have one. If they pay me, I will. I can't say anything else right now. Client confidentiality." She was pretty sure she could take payment. Her official certificate should arrive any day now.

"You should at least take time from your busy schedule to reply to Ralph's many attempts at communication."

"I know." She wouldn't tell her where she was headed. Definitely not. Not until there was more to report and, maybe, after the criminal was caught. Ralph would surely wrap that up soon. Saltlick wasn't very big. There were only a few choices of who would rob a place. The Yarborough twins were always at the top of any suspect list.

She retreated to the guest room where they had slept and got the notepad from her suitcase. At least she had thought to pack that. She would make her list. Or lists. Then call Ralph. It shouldn't take half an hour to do all of that.

Ten

By the time Immy got to the diner, it had been almost an hour. She missed a half hour by maybe fifteen or twenty minutes. If Long Hot Mike got impatient and gave up on her, that wouldn't be the worst thing in the world. She was cheating on Ralph. She really was. But she felt helpless to resist this guy. They didn't call him Hot Mike for nothing. She wondered if the Long was descriptive of anything, then gave herself a hard mental slap.

He hadn't given up on her. She was relieved and wasn't relieved about that. Okay, she was, but she should not be.

There he was, nursing a cup of coffee, and brightening up when he saw her. She made her way back to the booth, taking in the redolence of gravy, fried chicken, and biscuits. In fact, that's what both of them ordered.

Waiting for the food to come, Long turned serious. "There are a few things you should know," he said. "I know you're interested in what's going on around here. I've seen you talking to Loryetta."

"You have? Where?"

"Around." Had he seen her at the cemetery? No he'd been at the Henrys, unless he passed by on his way there.

"Well, yes, I'm curious. A man died. Murdered. Who wouldn't be curious about that? And, to tell you the truth, I'm kind of horrified. I mean, on his wedding day. Who would do that?"

"A lot of people probably wanted to. When we were in high school, he beat up a couple of guys a year younger."

"I've heard something about that," Immy said. "From Loryetta."

"She talked about that to you?"

"It shocked me, I'll tell you that. She seemed to think it was just fine to marry a guy like that."

Long looked at the floor beside their booth. "We were all a little wild back then. I did things I'm not proud of either. I outgrew that stuff. I don't do it anymore."

"Don't do what? Maim and kill people?" Were all the people in this town that way? Wild, reckless, and not seeing what was wrong with hurting other people?

He leveled a look at her with those gorgeous dark eyes. Were men supposed to have eyelashes like that, she wondered? "No, I don't. I didn't then, either. I just went along with Junior and Wyatt. It was a bad time."

"Loryetta told me Junior hasn't changed. He got in a bad fight a couple of months ago in another town near here and knifed a guy who still might die."

"He did, he did. It was horrible."

"And you and Wyatt were with him?"

Long looked away again. Maybe he wasn't quite as handsome as she'd thought.

"How is that different than when you were in high school? Have any of the three of you grown up at all?"

"We didn't know he was gonna do that! You know what else he did? After he stabbed the guy, when the cops came, he tried telling them that Wyatt did it, and then that I did it." His voice was rising with his heated words. "I wouldn't be a bit surprised if Wyatt's the one that killed him. With trying to blame him for that, and with Junior's daddy stealing the oil off his own daddy's land. Except Officer Herndon—he's my second cousin on my daddy's side—told me there was a big clue at the well. It's a cufflink that belongs to Eccles, Mr. Justice."

"Mr. Justice? Loryetta's father?" Even if he was a second cousin, the cop probably shouldn't tell Long that. No, she definitely shouldn't try to get info from the cousin.

"Yep. And he still held me there this morning. At the station. Me and Wyatt. For hours. Just cuz I left the bachelor party early. I didn't want to be so drunk and hungover on the day of the wedding. I hate having a hangover."

How early was early, Immy wondered. "Do the police think you and Wyatt had something to do with that other stabbing?"

"They do! They questioned both of us for hours about that. Then they hauled both of us in for this, too, asking if we killed Ned Junior. Can you believe that?"

It was Immy's turn to level a serious gaze at Long. "Did you?"

"Hell no!" He pounded the table so hard that some coffee jumped out of his mug. "But they need to keep questioning Wyatt!"

With that, he got up and ran out of the diner into the gathering darkness. Everyone watched him go, having heard his loud ranting. Immy grabbed a couple of paper napkins and mopped up his spill.

Among those watching, Immy noticed, was Sydney Harbor. The man who had been swindled and the father of Wyatt. That man was everywhere. He glared at Long, scratching the back of his hand. His hat was on the table and she couldn't see whether or not the feather was still there.

This was all muddled up, she was beginning to think. She had found a clue that might point to Mr. Harbor, or maybe Mr. Justice, who also had a big feather in his hat. Along with several other men at the reception. Was Mr. Harbor following her around? Well, no. He'd already been in the diner when she got there. She would have noticed if he'd come in after that. Maybe he was following Long. She would like to ask Long if he'd noticed being followed, but they were obviously not speaking right now.

Immy hadn't finished her meal, but didn't think she could with Mr. Harbor right there, two tables over, visibly seething about Long's accusation of his son. What kind of best buds *were* these guys? This one, Long, was eager to accuse both of the other two of things they probably did together. And now, he accused Wyatt of killing Junior.

She went out to her car and called Ralph. She was done with these local Lotharios.

He answered on the first ring. "Immy! Glad you answered. I tried to call you back."

"I know. I'm sorry. It's crazy here. The groom got killed the day of the wedding."

"Huh? The bride did him in?"

"No, he was killed before the wedding. Early in the morning, I think. It's just a mess. But the bride might hire me to find out who did it. I wish I had my—"

"That's what I've been calling about. You got a big envelope from the PI people. The ones you took that course from. Stangford Institute of Higher Learning."

She should not have ducked all those calls. She sucked in a big breath and held it, waiting for him to go on. He didn't. "What does it say?" She could picture that fancy letter *S* on the envelope. It had been that letter *S* that convinced her to take the online course.

"I didn't open it. It's addressed to you."

"Well open it! I give you official permission. I promise I won't charge you with a federal crime."

That made him laugh. It was so good to hear his laugh. She was glad she could make that happen. "That's a big relief. Okay, here goes." She could hear him working the envelope open, rattling some papers, probably pulling them out.

"How big is the envelope?"

"It's big. Big enough to hold this certificate. Congratulations. You're a certified Private Detective."

Now she wished she were back home. She would hug Ralph and kiss him, and go out with him and celebrate. "I passed? I passed my course?"

"With honors, it says. You know what this means, don't you?"

She shook her head, then remembered she was on the phone. "No, what does it mean, besides I passed and I'm certified? And I got a good score on the test."

"You're going to be twice the pain in the ass you've always been when something goes on around here."

"Can you see my grin? You know I will. You got that right. What's happening with the library? Did the twins do it?"

"No, they're in jail for something else."

"Tough break."

"They stole a car and crashed it."

Immy shook her head. "So who do you think robbed the library? And why? You said they didn't take any books."

"It must have been someone who thinks libraries collect a lot more in overdue fines than they do."

"They stole money?"

"They did. Only one person. He did."

"How much did he get?"

Ralph laughed. It was so good to hear that again. "Five dollars and seventy-five cents."

"Crooks really are dumb, aren't they?" Her phone buzzed. "I think I have another call. I'll call you later tonight and we can talk. Okay?" She was so done with these local boys. Ralph was worth ten of any of them.

The call was from Hortense, who said that Lulu was serving fried chicken with biscuits and gravy in a few minutes. Good, she could get the meal she had just ordered and paid for. And couldn't eat. In fact, she'd paid for two of them since Long Tuttle had stormed out leaving her holding the bill.

Eleven

EVERYONE AROUND THE TABLE WAS FULL, or "replete," as Hortense said. Replete with chicken fried inside the most delicate breading crust, biscuits so light they almost floated, and gravy heavy enough to hold all of that down. There was also a token salad, to give the appearance of a healthy meal. Everyone had a bit of that, too.

Immy had placed her hands on the sides of her chair and leaned forward, to scoot her chair back and leave the table, when Lulu said, "Don't anybody leave. There's banana pudding."

Someone groaned. Immy hoped it wasn't her. When she tasted the magical creamy concoction, she discovered she wasn't nearly as full as she thought she was.

"Mommy, can you know how to make this?" Drew asked.

"Can she learn how to make it?" Hortense was determined her granddaughter speak properly, after all.

"Can you, Mommy?"

"Sure she can." Lulu beamed at the empty pudding bowls around the table. "I'll give her the recipe."

That wouldn't guarantee Mommy would learn how to make it, though. Immy had a lot of recipes that didn't work for her like they did for her mother. "Maybe Geemaw can make it."

"Can you, Geemaw?"

Hortense could never resist those bright eyes. "Of course. With a high degree of certitude, it is possible that I can."

"Can I play with Babalu now?" Drew flitted on to the next topic in her mind. Given permission, she ran out the back door.

"It's too bad we can't have him in the house," Lulu said. "He's so small. I kind of hate to leave him out. But he's not housetrained."

"Do you think a hawk will get him?" Immy asked. "Or a coyote?"

Lulu shuddered. "Maybe."

Victor patted her shoulder. "I can make him a shelter."

Lulu, and everyone else, agreed that it was a swell idea. Victor headed out to the yard to get started on his project right away. Immy wondered if he would build it in the next couple of hours. She also wondered if he had the material.

She wandered out after him to see him pulling planks of wood from behind the shed. He did have the material. He had set up a lantern to work in the dusk. Maybe he would have it finished by the end of the day. He seemed awfully capable.

The little goat trotted up to her and gave her a tiny head butt against her leg. When he turned his face up to her, she had a momentary startle at the eyes, then gazed into them. Babalu gazed back at her. Maybe she could get used to them. The rest of him was so darn cute.

Later, helping with the dishes, Immy was alone with Lulu in the kitchen.

"What happened when you found Ned Junior? I mean how did you notice him?" The pumpjack had been the one that was the closest one to their house, but it wasn't that close. Quite a bit of mesquite grew between the backyard and the oil field. "You left the church and found him?"

"Victor hadn't wanted to go to the wedding in the first place. When everything was delayed so long, I couldn't keep him there and we came home. We were out back and we just noticed something the wrong color. When the arm came up, we saw him above the brush. That black suit and the white shirt. They stood out."

That made sense. "Could you tell right away that he was dead?"

"Why are you asking these questions? Why do you want to know about that? It's gruesome."

"Just curious." She wasn't going to mention her Case. If it was a Case. But now she wondered why Lulu didn't want to answer questions. Could she and Victor have had anything to do with his death? What would their motive be? They were close enough to the family to be invited to the wedding, but most of the town must have been. The families of the bride and groom seemed to have a lot of enemies, having swindled so many of their neighbors. She would have to check to see if the top of that crossbeam was actually visible from their backyard.

"It's just so awfully gruesome. I wish we hadn't found him."

Immy remembered that she hadn't told anyone about her certification. "I have something happier to talk about. Ralph, back home, called me today and told me I passed my course to become a private detective. I'm official." She beamed with her news.

Lulu made a face. "Why do you want to do that? Are you so very fascinated with awful things?"

Another person who just didn't get it. "No, not that. I like to help people solve problems. When there are questions about things that happened, people need to have their questions answered."

"And you think you can do that?"

"Yes, I do. I know I can. I've done some of it in the past."

Lulu shook her head. "Such foolishness."

The dishes were all washed, rinsed, and dried, so Immy left the kitchen and went out back to play with the goat and the dogs with Drew, and to watch Victor start to hammer together a crude shed. She did try to see the pumpjack from the yard, any part of it. But it was dark now and she couldn't see much out there in the unlighted oil field. She could certainly hear the machinery, creaking rhythmically, with undertones of clanking for percussion, with Victor's hammering for variety. The goat had a peculiar odor, but it wasn't too bad outdoors. And she caught a whiff of the awful sulfur smell again that went with oil wells. She would never see anything here tonight. It was full dark now. She had to get out there during the day, out to the crime scene.

But, even going out to the pump again, what would she find that the police couldn't? They even had a cufflink linking, as it were, Loryetta's dad to the crime. She had so many questions. Was it the only cufflink in the world like that? Did others have cufflinks that were similar? How would a person lose a cufflink strangling someone and climbing up to tie the body to the crossbeam? If he was strangled. She was picturing it that way for some reason.

She wandered out of the yard, into the oil field, for privacy from Victor, Drew, and Babalu. She got to the nearest pump. Holding her arms out, she strangled an imaginary person in front of her. Nope, that didn't involve her sleeves. The next step was putting him up there. She looked up at the structure, relentlessly bobbing up and down, stroke after stroke after stroke. It looked so much like a giant insect. She knew it was just a machine, but she had seen people paint faces on the front part, the part that looked like a head. She had even seen antennae fastened onto them to make them look more like giant grasshoppers. Her nose started running from being this close to the fumes and she swiped at it with the back of her hand.

No one could carry a body up there—no one could even reach that place without a ladder. Not alone, anyway.

She turned on her phone's flashlight and looked for marks that a ladder may have made in the dirt, close to the thing. The ground was completely trampled. Was this the actual scene of the crime?

If there had been holes made by the legs of a ladder, they were obscured now. Giving the pump one more good look, and finding nothing else, she went back to the yard, where Victor had already finished the goat shed. That should have been an all-day project, she thought. At least. He was awfully handy.

They were gathered in front of it.

Drew was trying to coax the little goat inside, but he wanted nothing to do with it, hopping and jumping away when she tried to lead him.

"That's okay, Drew," Victor said. "I'll go get something to tempt him, then we can shut him in there for the night, so he'll be safe."

Victor ran inside and returned quickly with a couple of carrots.

"Do baby goats like carrots?" Drew asked. "Can their little teeth chew them?"

"Babalu isn't a baby," he said. "He's just very small. This is as big as he can get."

Drew gave the goat a sad look. "Poor little thing." To her, growing big was a virtue. She had been doing it, and getting congratulated for her inches, her whole short life. Drew tilted her head and gave Babalu a look of pure pity. The eyes didn't bother Drew at all.

Immy laughed. "He's okay. He likes being that size. If he were bigger, he wouldn't fit inside his new house." Of course, she thought, he might not need one if he were full sized.

Sure enough, it worked. Victor showed the carrots to Babalu, then threw them inside. The little guy trotted in, nice as you please, and Victor closed the door he had put on the shelter. It even had a crude latch, made with pieces of wood.

"That's a nice job," Immy told him. "It's perfect. You're very handy."

"I have to be, making everything in the house look like 1950, when you can't buy a lot of that stuff anymore."

"I suppose that's true." She wondered if he had a ladder. And rope. He looked strong enough to carry another man up a ladder and lash him onto a crossbeam, if anybody did.

Twelve

The next day was Sunday, the day after the wedding. The day that had seemed to go on forever. Everyone woke fairly early. Immy lay in bed longer than the rest, but the smell of bacon and cinnamon toast drew her to the kitchen in time to eat with everyone else.

"Do y'all want to go to church with us?" Lulu asked.

Immy noticed that she and Victor were already dressed for it, she in a pant suit and he in a regular man's suit, probably the same one he'd worn yesterday. Men's suits all looked the same to her, except the double-breasted ones. She tried to imagine being there again, in the place where the disastrous wedding had not happened. It made her shiver a bit.

"We would be delighted to attend in your company," Hortense answered. "What is the time of departure?"

"Oh, we go to the late service. It doesn't start until eleven."

Immy glanced at the clock on the wall. It had large numbers and was encased in red plastic. It went with the theme of the house nicely. It also told her that it was ten o'clock right then. That didn't seem like a lot of time.

"I don't know if we can get ready by then," she said, not wanting to go.

"Of course you can, Imogene. You merely need to finish your morning repast and don the clothing you brought for either the rehearsal dinner or the wedding."

Immy shuddered again at the memory of both of them. "I don't think I feel very well today. I'll stay home."

"Very well. Then you had better get clothing onto Nancy Drew so she will not be tardy."

With a sigh, she got up, summoned Drew, and went into the bedroom to dress her. She knew her mother saw right through her, but was thankful she wasn't calling her out, insisting that she go, calling attention to how overly sensitive she was, in Hortense's view. Immy had to agree with her mother sometimes about that.

There was a flurry for the next half hour or so. The dogs and the goat had to be fed and everyone had to get dressed. All but Immy. She said she would do the dishes after they left, but Lulu told her not to if she was feeling sick. That made her feel guilty, since she wasn't a bit sick. But she didn't feel guilty enough to admit she was just fine and didn't want to revisit that place. To be honest, that might make her sick. It was just too sad.

After the house was quiet, she wondered if she could get in contact with Loryetta about the Case. Or would Loryetta be at the church? She thought probably not. Surely Loryetta would be a lot more averse to re-entering the place than Immy was.

She called and Loryetta answered right away. "Hi," Immy said, as brightly as she could. "Have you had a chance to talk to your dad?"

"They let me see him for a few minutes kind of late last night." She sounded like she'd been crying. Or maybe was still crying right now. He must be locked up still.

"Did you, you know, talk to him about, you know, having me look into things?"

"Oh gosh, I completely forgot. I was so rattled seeing him like that. In jail. With guards all around while we talked. Immy, it's terrible."

"I'm sure it is. It must be awful for all of you."

"I've been out of my mind. I can't do anything except sit on the couch and stare, except when I'm crying."

Did Immy want to work on this? What if she found that the guy was guilty, that he had killed Ned Junior? They wouldn't like that. It would be unlikely they would pay her. The damning clue came to mind, the one Long Hot Mike had mentioned.

Immy was sitting on the bed in the guest room and idly opened the top dresser drawer. "Do you know anything about a cufflink?"

"Uh, no. Except that Daddy said he lost one at the church. Did somebody find it?"

He lost it at the church? If that were true, did someone else pick it up and plant it at the site to frame him? How could she resist untangling this? Her curiosity was ramped to the max. She needed to find out what was going on.

"Well, as soon as you know, give me a call and I can start to work trying to clear him." A framed picture of a young boy lay in the drawer. It looked old. It was a color picture, but faded. She put it down carefully and quickly closed the drawer. She had no business looking in there.

"Oh gosh, Immy. Do you really think you can?"

"I…I don't know yet. But maybe." If someone had framed him, that would give her a place to start, a foothold. She needed to clear him, since he was her client.

"Let me think about this. And I'll try to talk to Daddy. I'll call you back."

Here she was, alone in the house, except for all of these animals. The four dogs had been left inside. What was she going to do for the next hour? Her cell phone answered that question for her. It was Ralph.

"Can you talk?" he asked.

"I can. And I need to. Need to talk to you."

"You're not at church?"

"I couldn't do it. Everyone else went, but it's too horrible. It's the place where the bride and groom were supposed to have the happiest moment in their lives. Well, one of the happiest. And then we found out he was dead. It really killed the moment. Everyone was feeling down. It's just too…too horrible, too…"

"What exactly is going on out there?"

She told him. She started with her conversation with Loryetta in the bathroom the day before the wedding, when she was expressing doubts about marrying Ned Junior. She told Ralph why, that it was because he might go to prison if the guy he stabbed died.

"She wasn't going to call it off just because he was the kind of person who stabs people, but she would if he had to go to prison."

"Really? She doesn't mind marrying a bar fighter? I guess a lot of women do marry them. They aren't all single." Maybe he knew a lot of guys like that. She didn't.

"Her main concern, honestly, was that she was afraid it would reflect badly on her daddy. And Mother had already told me the daddy is a low life. His partner is the crook who is married to her cousin. They've been swindling people out of their oil rights when they buy land from him. Him and the groom's father, together. Then the groom ended up dead on the morning of the wedding. The body was found not too far from where we're staying, with these people that have a house from the Lucille Ball show."

"Immy, could you please come home now?"

She let out a breath. "I can't. I might have a Case."

"What? What are you talking about? Are you sick?"

"No, a Case. A Case to solve. I don't have a name for it yet."

"Someone is paying you to find the killer?"

"Well, maybe."

"And who would that be?"

"The bride."

"The woman who would have been the bride."

"Yes, her daddy is locked up for killing the groom."

"Immy, that's all messed up. Way too messed up. You need to get away from there."

"I know. But I'm not sure he did it. Why would a man kill his daughter's groom the day of the wedding? They dote on each other, the daddy and the bride. I don't think he would hurt her that way."

"Maybe he didn't want her marrying that kind of guy."

"I think he's the same kind."

"Immy, come home! Get away from those people!"

"We might be home soon. If they don't hire me, we'll leave. But tell me about your Case."

"I don't have a Case, Immy, not the way you do, with a name and all. I'm a cop, not a PI."

"Okay, your investigation. The library heist."

She heard an audible sigh. Maybe she shouldn't use the word "heist" for a small robbery in Saltlick.

"Immy, we're not spending a lot of time and resources on this. But we did find out that there are a couple of Yarborough boys in Dallas."

"Boys?"

"No, adults. As opposed to the local Yarborough twins. They might have been visiting here recently."

If only she were in Saltlick, she could investigate that.

"Look, you have to come home. Now. Today. That's all there is to it."

"Oh, I have to go. Talk to you later, Ralph. Love you."

She didn't have to go, but she did have to end that conversation before he talked her into leaving.

It was still at least a half an hour until the rest of them came home from church, depending on how long-winded the sermon was. There was certainly plenty that needed to be preached to these people. Did they ever listen to the sermons, though?

She got some dog treats and a carrot—there were a lot of them in the crisper—and led the dogs outside. Two of them piddled, but the other two didn't seem to need to. They all did a few tricks when she asked, treats in hand. But Babalu knew she had a carrot and kept butting in. Literally. Those little horns on his head were solid. Once or twice he knocked the carrots out of her hands, onto the ground, and when she bent over, wham! She might be quite bruised on her rear end.

"Hey, little goat. Do you do tricks? Can you stand on your hind legs?" She lifted the carrot up high. His face was so cute, in spite of the pupils. The little guy craned his neck as far as it would go, but his hooves didn't leave the ground. "Can you sit? Sit! Sit!" She pointed to the ground with vigor in her finger. Apparently he didn't do that either. So she gave him the carrot. He didn't butt her again, which was good. Carrots were his drugs. After he munched the crunchy vegetable, he mellowed out and lay on the grass. He'd been extremely animated all the other times she'd seen him.

She did learn one thing in the yard. You could clearly see that pumpjack arm going up and down. Well, you could see it when it went up. If a body were tied to it and it was daylight, you would be able to see it. And run and report it to the police.

It wasn't long before she heard the two vehicles out front. And very soon after that, Drew was in the backyard with her, clothes changed and another carrot in her hand. Immy wondered if too many carrots were bad for goats.

Thirteen

Everyone settled into something that afternoon. Lulu had to get a start on a Christmas stocking for Babalu. She had apparently hand-knitted one for Victor and one for each of the four dogs. Immy spied the pile of them beside her where she sat in a comfy turquoise chair—or a chair as comfy as the square 1950s furniture got—and started clicking her needles together. The stocking for the little goat was going to be green. It kind of clashed with the chair.

Drew and her grandmother retreated to the guest room, which had a fairly nice, wide chair—plenty big enough to hold both of them—to read a book together.

Victor headed for the backyard. Immy, at loose ends, followed him. He pulled two boards from the shed, got out two sawhorses and a hand saw, and started measuring something on the goat shed.

"Are you going to give him another room?" she asked, expecting him to realize that was just a silly, idle question.

"Kind of. I think he needs a porch. There aren't any windows in his house, so he might need a place to shelter where he can see out. I'll probably cut some windows later."

That was…kind of odd, but nice. In an odd way. "He's such a lucky little goat."

She watched him for a few minutes, then realized he might be a source of some information. He'd lived here his whole life.

"How well do you know Mr. Justice? And Mr. Newberry? Are they about your age?"

"They're a couple of years older than me. Them and Sydney. Yeah, we know each other. That's why we were invited to the wedding."

"And the rehearsal dinner."

"At least that went well, the way it was supposed to."

"Not for Mr. Harbor."

"No, I guess Sydney got upset. Can't blame him. Them rubbing his face in his mistake like that. But it's easy to see how he could buy property and not ask about mineral rights. If you use a real estate agent, they're supposed to know about those things." Victor shook his head, then took another measurement and started sawing the second board.

"He didn't use an agent?"

"Who does that? They're expensive. But he paid for it in the long run. It was a hard lesson. He's not the only one swindled by them."

"Do you think he killed Junior Newberry?"

He thought for a moment. "I can't see it. What good would that do him? He probably wanted to kill Ned."

"That's Junior's father, right?"

"Yep. Him and Eccles, they were both running their schemes, but I think it's Eccles that Sydney bought that parcel from."

"I've heard some things about their sons from Loryetta. They all three seem to be hell raisers. Well used to be."

"Their papas were just as bad. Worse. I've always stayed away from them as much as I could."

"Who do you think could have killed Ned Junior?"

"Hard to say. He's hurt a lot of people, just like his daddy."

There seemed to be more motive for killing the elder Mr. Newberry. She had an inspiration, remembering what the two men looked like. What if Ned was the intended victim?

"Do you think somebody thought Junior was his father? Thought they were killing Mr. Newberry?"

Victor looked up and squinted at the sky. He took a couple of deep, slow breaths. "Could be, I suppose. They would look pretty much the same size in the dark. They were both all dolled up for the ceremony."

"One more thing bothers me. Why would he be killed way out there? Behind your house?"

Now he squinted at her. Did he think she was accusing him?

She continued. "I mean, he wouldn't be here, would he? He'd be at his own house or the church."

"Can't say. Them old boys and their kin are always checking on their wells." He started sawing with all his might.

It was apparent that he wanted to end this conversation, so Immy wandered back inside the house. On the way, however, she wondered if Victor was casting suspicion on the other two men for his own reasons. What was his history with them? Or with Ned Junior, if there was one? Maybe Lulu would be more forthcoming about that.

Immy took a seat in front of Lulu on the nearby hard, round ottoman, in matching turquoise, of course. Her mother and daughter seemed to be in the bedroom reading still. Unless her mother had fallen asleep. She would have to check on Drew pretty soon.

"You're really good at that," she told Lulu, starting in easy.

"Oh, it's not hard. This is just a plain knit stitch. I don't do any fancy ones."

"I was just talking to Victor and he told me about you finding Ned Junior out there." Not quite true, but they had talked about Junior.

Lulu slammed her eyes shut. "It was horrible."

"What do you reckon he was doing out there?"

"Immy, we talked about this already. I really don't want to anymore."

"I'm sorry. I just can't understand. It doesn't make any sense. Did you know Ned Junior very well?"

"Look at this town." She set her knitting in her lap and stared at Immy. "It's not a big place. Everyone knows everyone." Immy could tell she was getting annoyed.

"But Sydney managed to get swindled, so he didn't know enough about Eccles and Ned."

"Well, he should have, by then! Everybody else did." She took a breath and picked up her knitting again, seeming more composed. "Sydney keeps to himself too much. He's kind of a hermit."

"Victor said they all three ran around together when they were younger."

"They did. And they terrorized everyone. Just like their sons do now. Well, I guess Junior won't bother anybody anymore. Wyatt and Long will have to terrorize on their own now."

"So, you and Victor don't have any kids?"

Lulu's lips tightened. "No, we don't."

That seemed to be a sore subject for her. They must have wanted them, but couldn't. "You reckon someone had it in for Junior?"

"Could be anyone." She turned her shoulder slightly to exclude Immy. She wasn't talking about this anymore, that was plain.

Did she and Victor have something to do with his death? They didn't seem to have much connection to him, but they also didn't want to give her much information. She would shift to another tactic for now. Maybe she should find out more about the guys that had been hurt by the younger trio. But not here, not from Lulu or Victor.

Why wasn't Loryetta calling her back? Should she try to call Eccles, the woman's father? Was he still in jail?

After checking up on her mother and Drew—Hortense was snoring none too softly, slumped in the large-ish chair, and Drew was playing on the floor with some stuffed animals she had brought—Immy told everyone she needed to run an errand.

Fourteen

Would the jail be open? It wasn't that late yet, although it was Sunday. But wasn't a jail open every day? The one in Saltlick was. She got the keys to the van and headed to the police department. It was kind of around the corner from the main street, in back of the City Hall. The front door opened when she pulled on it, so that was good. A man sat at a window in the small lobby. He didn't look up when she came in.

"Excuse me?"

"You want something?" He wore a police uniform.

Well, why else would I be here, she wanted to say. No, just passing by and thought I'd come in? She swallowed her sarcasm. There was that uniform. She didn't want to make him mad. "I was wondering if I could talk to Mr. Justice."

"Eccles? He's in jail."

"I know. That's why I came here."

"No ma'am, you can't see him. You're not on the list."

"How do you know?"

He huffed at her. "I know everybody on the list. And you ain't one of 'em."

"Okay. But could I get on the list?"

Now he frowned. Policemen always looked so severe when they frowned. "No ma'am."

"Who gets on the list? Do PIs get on it?"

"You a PI?" His disbelief was obvious. He even made a barking, laughing sound.

"I am."

"Show me your papers."

"I…I don't have them with me."

He shook his head. "Go away and don't bother me."

That was awfully rude. And dismissive. "Well, could I just ask you a couple of questions about his case?"

He didn't say no, so she did. "What has he been charged with? When is his arraignment?" Those were questions a reporter would ask, it occurred to her. She should have told him she was a reporter. But she wouldn't have been able to prove that, either.

Now he squinted. He was using up his whole array of tough cop faces. "I can't tell you any of that."

She wasn't sure that was true. It was time to switch tactics. "Can you tell me about what happened in, um, Hillstown?" She thought she had the name of the place where Ned Junior knifed the guy right.

"I don't see how that would hurt anything."

"Who was it who got attacked?"

"Guy's name was Clayton Barrelson."

"Was? He died?"

"Just this morning. If Junior was still alive, he'd be gettin' charged right about now."

"Clayton Barrelson. He lived in Hillstown?"

"Born and raised. His ma and pa are still there. A slew of cousins and other kin, too. I reckon it'll be a big funeral."

"Was another guy injured that night?"

"He was, but he's okay. The woman was only slightly injured."

"Do you know when the funeral will be?"

"Why? You want to go to the funeral?"

Kind of. She could scout out suspects, of course. But she couldn't say that. He should have thought of that himself. But, if they knew who killed him, there wouldn't really be suspects. Okay, she had that straight. "Thanks for your help." She turned and left. She could get the rest of the information she needed somewhere else. *If* she got hired. Maybe she should be keeping track of the hours she was putting in. And the mileage, though there wasn't much of that yet. She didn't know how far away Hillstown was, but she would find out.

She walked out of the jail and looked around. It wasn't that big. Could she figure out where Eccles Justice was and talk to him through the window? The solid brick building didn't have any windows on the side where she was. Nor on the side facing the cross street. They had to be around back. She crept through the parking lot and ducked between the cars to get to the back. The parking lot had three empty Slap Out Police cars parked in it. In case they had those alarms when you got close, she skirted them by quite a bit.

Sure enough, there were three small, high windows on that side. Maybe there were only three cells. Saltlick had two, and this town wasn't much bigger. There was a large metal trash bin at the end of the wall. If she could stand on that, she could maybe see inside the cells. She tried to shove it, but it wouldn't budge, even when she put her shoulder up against it and threw her whole body weight behind her push. Now what? Could she drive the van up to one of these windows?

As she stood thinking about it, visually trying to measure exactly how high those windows were, a heavy hand tapped her shoulder. When she whirled around, the officer who had been inside towered over her. She hadn't realized he was so tall when he'd been sitting.

"Yes, sir?" she asked, hoping he couldn't tell what she'd been trying to do.

"You don't think we have security cameras outside the jail?"

He pointed up to the corner of the building. It sure did look like a security camera.

"I thought I heard a…cat back here. I had to come and check it out."

"What you have to do right now, missy, is get in your car and drive away."

That did seem like a good idea, so she did.

Fifteen

"WHERE HAVE YOU BEEN?" Hortense was in the living room watching a quiz show when Immy returned from her aborted mission.

"Just driving around. It's a nice little town."

Hortense frowned. Immy knew she didn't think the town was nice at all, and she knew Immy didn't think so either. "We should probably drive home tomorrow."

Immy's shoulders dropped. They might have to. Maybe she wasn't going to get the job. She shuffled into the kitchen where she found a plate of warm chocolate chip cookies. Lulu was right there, taking another batch out of the oven, so she asked, "Are these for us?"

"Yes, I thought your little girl would like them. Go ahead, help yourself."

At least she wasn't annoyed with Immy anymore. And she liked Drew. Immy picked one up and took it to the backyard. Drew was there, running around with Babalu. She couldn't quite tell, but she thought that Babalu was enjoying it. The little guy jumped straight up sometimes, managing to kick his back legs out at the same time. Immy thought it was quite acrobatic. Drew tried to imitate him, but couldn't, probably because she only had two legs.

The clanking of the oil pumps seemed louder, the darker it got.

"Babalu likes cookies," Drew called when she saw her mom with one. Were cookies good for goats? They ate almost everything, so it was probably fine.

Dusk was gathering and soon all she could see of the goat were the white parts on his face and feet. That face and those feet were never still, moving a mile a minute. She was starting to feel the mosquitoes, too.

"Let's go in before we get eaten up," she called to Drew. Maybe she wouldn't be too sad to leave this place. To not have a Case. There was nothing pretty about it. It was flat and dry, and downright ugly where the oil field was. The salt water that got pumped out to drill a well killed all the grass and trees, she knew. She glanced at the top of the nearest pump as it rose above the mesquite. It was still light enough to see it. No bodies were on it.

She brushed cookie crumbs from Drew's shirt before they came inside. She couldn't see, but assumed she had had some. Victor was coming out to put Babalu in his safe little house.

"Victor? Is it okay if Drew gave cookies to Babalu?"

He grinned at Drew. "Did you do that? That was nice of you." Then looked at Immy. "I think it's fine. They're little garbage cans, you know."

She did know, but wanted to ask. Her phone beeped. Drew had already gone inside, and the caller ID was Ralph. She sat on a step of the back porch to take the call.

"Hey, how are you doing?"

"Immy, I want you to come home. I don't like you being there."

"We might come home tomorrow. Or the next day." If she could put Hortense off one more day. "It doesn't look like Loryetta will hire me."

"I miss you so much. The bed is empty when you're not in it."

Aw, that was sweet. And a better tactic than ordering her around. "I miss you, too, Ralphie." She really did. But…if she could get a Case. Her very first as a real PI.

She moved over a bit so Victor could get past her to go inside the house.

"Could you do me a huge favor?" she asked.

"Sure, anything. Well, I mean…"

Before he could rethink his rash statement, she asked him to photograph her new diploma and send that to her.

"I guess I could. But you're not going to need it there."

"I know," she lied. "I just want to see it for myself. And to have it on my phone."

He reluctantly snapped it and sent it.

Ping! There it was.

Ping! There was also a call from Loryetta.

"Thanks, babe. I better go get Drew into the bathtub."

"Yeah, big drive tomorrow."

She sent a smooching sound and switched over to Loryetta's call. The sound of retching greeted her. "Just a minute!" Loryetta yelled.

She was soon back on the line, after the sound of the toilet flushing.

"Okay, here I am. Sorry about that. I can't tell when it's gonna happen."

"Are you sick? Did you just get sick today?"

"Not exactly sick. I'm pretty sure I'm pregnant. Mama called Aunt Luralene when I first puked this morning and that's what they decided. Aunt Luralene isn't very happy with me. Well, Mama isn't either."

"Oh. Oh no. That's not too good." It was pretty bad. Being pregnant and the guy being dead. Like a war widow or something.

"I know. I feel so sick."

Immy didn't think her feeling sick was the bad part, but she didn't say so. The woman wasn't thinking too much ahead right then, Immy thought. If she ever did.

"Listen, I finally talked to Daddy and he wants you to look around for other people who might've killed Neddie. He swears he didn't do it."

Immy's mouth dropped open. Really? She was getting a Case? It took her a few seconds to regain her ability to speak. "YES. Ahem, yes, I can do it. Would he like to see a copy of my certificate?"

"Yeah, probably. He says to bring a contract to the jail and he'll sign it."

A contract! Now she would have to figure out what to write in a contract. "I'll be over in the morning, if that's okay."

"Sure, he wasn't thinking you'd come tonight. You know what? Wait until I call you. His arrangement thing is tomorrow, so he thinks he might get out."

Arraignment, Immy was pretty sure, was what she meant. Now she would have to drive to Hillstown to look up the family of the guy Ned Junior killed. "How about tomorrow afternoon? I have to be put on the list.”

Loryetta didn't ask how Immy knew that. “Sure. Just wait till I call you and then we'll see where everything is.”

“And where everybody is.”

As soon as she hung up with Loryetta, she called her PI boss, Mike Mallett.

“Immy? Do you know what time it is?”

She didn't. “It's nighttime, I guess. It's dark out.”

“It's Sunday night. What do you want?” His voice, always raspy, was croaking right now. Maybe he was tying one on tonight. That had been known to happen.

“I need a favor.”

“Sure you do.”

“I got my diploma. I'm a PI now. And I need to know how to write a contract for a case.”

“Are you sure? You got something that says you're certified?”

“I graduated from my course.”

“Yeah, but you ain't got the government license, do you?”

She wasn't sure. “It might be included. I can send you a copy.”

She could hear him scoffing. “You do that. I thought you were at a wedding.”

“I am. I was. The groom was murdered.”

“No shit. They want you to find out who did it? Where is this Podunk town that they can't figure that out? I bet it was either the bride or her father.”

It was all she could do to keep from pointing out that the Podunk town of Wymee Falls gave him plenty of work, even with a perfectly good police department. “I just need to know how to write a contract.”

“Sure, kiddo. I'll text you something tomorrow. I assume you don't need it right now. Even though you interrupted my weekend to ask for it right now.”

“You're right. Just trying to get a head start on the week. Thanks so much.”

Things were going well. It shouldn't take too long to find another good suspect, gather clues and nail him, and get back home.

Sixteen

No one wanted to go to Hillstown with her the next morning. Hortense was adamant that she wanted to head home to Saltlick.

"Mother, I've just been hired to do an investigation." They were in the Henrys' kitchen, eating breakfast.

"Surely not." Hortense paused in bringing the bit of sausage to her mouth.

Immy was hurt at her obvious disbelief. She reached for her phone and pulled up the picture of her diploma. It did say "certificate," so maybe she was a real, honest-to-goodness PI, without need for any further proof. "I got this in the mail at home. Ralph sent me this. And Loryetta called me last night. Her daddy wants to hire me. He didn't kill Ned Junior, so they want me to find out who did." She leaned over to show the phone screen to her mother.

Her mother's glance at this extremely important document was extremely brief. "Imogene, you know better than that. Every person who is in a correctional institution has been incarcerated unjustly, if you listen to what they, themselves, say."

She did know that. "Mother, he's not incarcerated. I mean, not even convicted. He's only in jail and he's probably getting out right now since his arraignment is this morning."

"Why are you not present for that?"

"Well, lawyers do that, not PIs." This was something her mother did not know and she did. Amazing.

"I surmise that is true. Is there some method by which you could remain here and Nancy Drew and I could return to our domicile?"

"I can't think of any."

Lulu Henry had been listening to them, since she was sitting with them at the kitchen table, finishing up the breakfast Hortense had made for everyone. "You know, I wouldn't mind if you stayed a few more days. Hortense, you could show me what you did to those eggs that made them so fantastic." She tried to scrape one more bite from her empty plate.

Hortense beamed and almost tittered. Lulu had found the way to her heart. There wasn't much she liked better than having folks appreciate her cooking. "I could certainly demonstrate my methods to you. They are not particularly difficult."

Immy breathed a sigh of relief. It would all be okay. Hortense would gladly stay and Immy could run around solving her Case. She ducked her head down to hide her smile at how that had turned out. She knew Drew would gladly play with the goat for a few more days, too.

Soon, she was on the road, on the job. The drive to Hillstown was pleasant. The vast Texas sky was a pure blue today, with gentle puffs of white clouds wandering by. Scrubby trees lined the two-lane road, with occasional ranch houses set back from the road. She drove past a small, well-kept cemetery flying an American flag. It looked downright cheerful compared to the one in Slap Out, where she'd met Loryetta. Some of the land was obviously farmed, but fallow this time of year, waiting for next year's crops, with the reddish soil lying bare in neat, plowed rows. Other fields held grazing cattle, serenely chomping grass and chewing cuds. It was hard to believe any violence could occur anywhere around here.

After about a half an hour, a water tower signaled her approach to the town. The houses clustered more closely together, neat one-story brick and siding dwellings. She passed a small excavation company, where they dug gravel to make cement, according to the sign. She also passed a junkyard. The kinds of establishments that were just outside small towns. A bank, a school, and a church signaled her arrival at the outskirts. She pulled into a gas station to fuel the van and to reconnoiter.

The drive had been so lovely. She tried to think how long it had been since she had driven somewhere all by herself, at her own pace, with her own radio station, the window cracked just as she liked it, to let a small breath of air waft past her face, while the heater blasted from the floor, keeping her feet warm. It pleased her that she would have one more drive like this when she returned to Slap Out.

But for now, what was she doing? She had a name. She had no contacts, no address. She got out of the van to get gasoline, as long as she was here. This was the usual, do-it-yourself place she was used to. When her tank was full and paid for, she pulled away from the pump into a parking place next to the small cement-block building and started working her phone. She opened the app that Mike Hammer used when he tracked down people. It wasn't exactly clear whether or not she should be using it when she wasn't working for him, but it was functioning for her. When she typed in Claude Barrelson and the town, nothing came up, so she left off his first name. Maybe he had lived with his parents. That gave her better results. There were two addresses in this town.

Now, how would she approach this? It probably wasn't the best idea to say she was sorry for their son's death and then let them know that she wanted to see if they had killed Ned Newberry, Jr., to avenge him. No, she would have to use subterfuge, the PI's tool.

The first address was listed to a Gantry Barrelson. She drove to a split-level that looked like it had been built a few decades ago. It was still in good shape, and the front yard held indications that a prolific flowerbed had flourished in the summer.

Her knock was answered by a short, stout woman with bags hanging far below her dull gray eyes, and wearing jeans and a sweatshirt with a picture of a hyena on it. Immy knew she had the animal right because it said *Hillstown Hyenas* above it. Texas towns had some odd high school mascots.

"Yes?" The bedraggled woman's voice was soft. She sounded defeated.

"Hello, ma'am. I'm looking for Gantry Barrelson."

"He's not here. He's picking out a coffin."

"I'm so sorry for your loss. Are you Claude's mother?"

Her expression hardened. "What do you want?"

"Mrs. Barrelson, I felt so bad when I read about your son, I wanted to offer my services."

"What services do you have? Who are you?"

"I represent a group of freelance charity writers and we can write a lovely obituary for you, if you haven't already done that." It sounded even more lame, saying it out loud here and now, than it had when she rehearsed it in her car a few minutes ago.

"Never heard of such a thing. The funeral home is helping with that. Who are you?"

"My name's Jane Dew." That was almost Jane Doe, so it should work. Immy/Jane stuck out her hand, but Mrs. Barrelson didn't take it.

She answered, though. "Minnie Barrelson. I think you should leave us alone." Taking a step back, she closed the door. At least she didn't slam it.

And now Immy knew who Claude's parents were. It was a step. A baby step.

Now she had to research these two, Gantry and Minnie. Maybe she could ask about them around town. She couldn't be Jane Dew for that, though, since she had used up that fake name for an obituary writer and such a person, if one existed, wouldn't be asking about them. Especially since she hadn't been hired.

She retreated to the van to think out her next step. She wished she had a good plan. She wished she had thought to bring a disguise, too. For the future, whenever she went on trips, she should be prepared to handle cases. She had passed a WellMart on the way into town. It might have some things she could use.

Forty-five minutes later she emerged from the huge store with a new notepad and package of pens, a short, red-headed wig, and a bright, shiny red cowgirl shirt with fringe. She would wear her own jeans and sneakers. Those were anonymous items. Cowgirl boots would have been nice, but they were pretty high-priced. She returned to the gas station she had used earlier and changed in the restroom, which had an outdoor entrance around the side.

Now, to find the local hangout and listen to gossip.

Seventeen

IT DIDN'T TAKE LONG CRUISING UP AND DOWN THE STREETS, before she found the place with the parking lot full of white pickups. She often wondered why Texans, especially men, preferred white pickups, since they always looked dirty, but maybe the standards of Texan pickup drivers weren't related to truck presentability and cleanliness.

When she entered the ice cream shop, across the street from a rather impressive shopping mall, she was glad to see that she wasn't the only female in the room. If the local hangout had been a bar, that might have been the case.

A woman was working behind the counter along with two teenage-looking boys, and two other women sat in a booth by a front window having shakes. Nevertheless, a lot of heads turned when she walked in. Probably the red wig, she figured, or the red shirt. She went to the counter to get a small vanilla cone, then took it to a booth near the two women. Her theory was that women were gossips and she would overhear the scuttlebutt there.

However, she mostly heard about the state of their own personal health and that of their husbands. When they started on the football accomplishments of their sons, she turned her concentration to the booth on the other side of her, cocking her head in that direction.

That yielded much better results. Four burly men were crowded onto the bench seats having burgers and fries. Except for the one who was having a burger and onion rings. Since she was facing them, they were a bit easier to overhear.

"You can't say they didn't expect that," one of them said.

"That's right. No way that boy was gonna live with all those injuries."

"Even if Gantry didn't expect him to live, you can't fault him for being torn up that he didn't make it."

She had struck pay dirt. Here was exactly the gossip she wanted to hear.

"You got that right. No one wants to bury a son."

Immy licked her cone slowly, waiting for them to get to the good parts. She didn't have to wait long.

"Did you hear that Gantry wants to pay a visit to that boy's daddy?"

"To that Newberry fella? What good is that gonna do him?"

"You got that right. There isn't anything gonna bring Claude back to life."

"Or Ned Junior. He's dead, too."

"Yeah, no good will come of Gantry driving over there. I saw him heading over there on my way here. He needs to stay here to get the funeral set up."

"Won't Minnie be doing that?"

"From what I hear, she's torn up worse than Gantry. Hasn't been out of the house in days."

"Gantry sure has been."

"What do you mean? I haven't seen him around."

"He drove out of town every day for about three days last week."

Which days? Immy was screaming inside. She had to know which days he drove to Slap Out.

"He had that cattle auction over to Mammoth, you know. I thought he coulda sent a hired hand."

Maybe he did, she thought. Maybe he didn't go to Mammoth. Maybe he went to Slap Out and killed Ned Junior.

"Aw, maybe that gave him something useful to do."

"You got that right. Don't you know he was good and ready to get out of the house? Must be awful depressing being inside with Minnie every day."

Immy heard murmurs of agreement. Her mind chewed on the information. Gantry, father of the young dead guy, had left the house a few times last week. Everyone thought he was going to a cattle auction. But was he? He very well could have been going to Slap Out to plan and carry out his revenge on Ned Junior for the death of his son. That would make perfect sense.

Now, how to verify that? How would she meet up with the elusive Gantry and ask him about the auction?

Aha. He was at the funeral home right now, they had said. She would waylay him when he came out.

It didn't take long to locate a funeral home, across the street from the liquor store. That seemed appropriate. Death gave people grief and grief made them drink. There were only two pickups in this parking lot. She wished she knew what kind of truck Gantry drove. When she noticed that one of them had a huge trailer hitch, she figured that one was his, for hauling a cattle trailer. She pulled the green van up next to it, wishing she had a white pickup so she would blend in and be less conspicuous.

She also wished she knew what Gantry looked like. As she waited for someone to come out, she pondered the two schemes she had thought of. One was to pretend to be a reporter doing a story on bar fights, since his son had gotten killed in one. The other was to pretend to be a reporter doing a story on people getting away with murder. That second one might be better. Surely he was sore about that. Maybe he would let something slip about avenging his son's death.

In less than ten minutes a man walked out of the double doors of the funeral parlor and stumbled down the steps. His face was wet. Immy knew the man had been crying and she couldn't blame him for that. But did she want to disturb him when he was in this state? The man could barely walk. When he reached his truck, he put a heavy hand on the hood to hold himself up.

After he had stood there, bowed, still leaning on the front of the truck, for a good few seconds, he pushed himself up and went to the door.

"Mr. Gantry?" Immy's question was as tentative as it could be. She didn't know if this was Mr. Gantry and, even if he was, if she should be pestering him. She had gotten out of the van and gone around the back of his truck.

He looked up, not hostile, just…maybe…puzzled. "Who are you?"

"My name is Jody Doe."

"Do I know you?"

"No sir, you do not. I'm a reporter for the TV station in a nearby town."

"Reporter?" He said that like it was a dirty word. "What town?"

She hadn't thought quite that far ahead. "Slap Out. Just down the road."

"I know damn well where Slap Out is. Didn't know it had a TV station."

Oh no! It probably didn't. "Just a small, local one. Mr. Gantry, my station is doing a series of stories on criminals who got away with their crimes. We thought that the unsolved murder of your son would be a good one to cover."

"Oh, you did, did you? It ain't unsolved. That damn Junior killed him. Everybody knows that."

"Yes, it's pretty certain that he did. But no one knows who killed Ned Newberry, Jr., your son's killer. Wouldn't you like to know who that person is?"

"So I can thank him and buy him a steak dinner? Sure. But I don't much care who did it. I care more that the bastard is dead. It would be fine with me if all three of the bastards were dead. Junior, Long, Wyatt. They're all trash. They all killed my son."

Those were the other members of the football team then. It made sense. "I can appreciate that, sir. Do you have any ideas on who could have killed Junior?"

He squinted at her, his leathery skin creasing at the corners of his eyes. "Don't you reckon they got him in jail? I heard they hauled in old man Justice for that."

"Yes, they did. But it's pretty certain he's not the killer." She wanted to see what effect that lie would have on the man.

It had a great effect. His face fell slack. "What the hell does that mean?"

"It means they think someone else must have done it." She was really totally making up a lot of things now. "Would you have any knowledge of someone else who could have done it?"

He took a menacing step toward her. "Are you accusing me of something?"

She stepped back. "No. No sir. No, I'm not. I just thought you might have heard something."

"Get out of my way." He climbed into the truck and backed it out, not looking to see if he was running over her or not. Luckily, she was ready, and he missed her toes by at least three inches. She ducked under his side mirror so it didn't take her head off.

Was that how a guilty man would act? She replayed their exchange, and realized he had said something that made her shiver, and that was that all three of them should be dead. If this man had killed Junior, would he kill the other two now?

What would her next step be? She had a disguise on and had a new fake name ready. Even a handy occupation. TV reporter. For a very small station. Could she make more use of this? She should find the scene of the crime, the first one. The bar where Ned Junior stabbed Claude. According to Long and others, anyway. Her GPS search showed that there were quite a few bars for a town this size. She decided to concentrate on the ones near the center of the town. The first one she came to was Friendly's Bar. This time of day, midmorning, only the serious drinkers were at it. A half dozen of them were slumped over the bar, one of them a woman. They didn't look too useful, so she concentrated on the bartender, a young dark-skinned guy who looked barely old enough to drink.

"What'll you have, ma'am?" His voice was soft and polite.

"Just a light beer. I'm so thirsty after driving all day."

"You on your way somewhere?" He pulled one of the levers and filled a glass for her.

"Yes, traveling through. You know, I heard something about a bad bar fight in this town awhile back. You remember a guy getting knifed?"

"Two guys. One just died."

"Yeah, I think my cousin knew him. She lived here a few years ago. Did that happen here, at your bar?"

He gave a soft laugh. "This ain't my bar, I just work here. But it didn't happen here. It was at Tex Mix. That's a rough place most nights. Lots of fights. But not that many stabbings. The whole town's upset about that. It was a gang of guys from another town. Bad dudes."

Immy was thrilled. She wouldn't have to order beers in a bunch of bars. That had been the main flaw in her plan, having to drink beer after beer to get information, and maybe not be able to drive back. Now she could zero in on the crime scene. She drank about a fourth of the glass, then left.

Should she continue her day-drinking investigation method or should she wait until a respectable time of day to be drinking? She hadn't wanted to spend a lot of time in this town this morning. But she was eager to find out more. So, continued day drinking, it was. Especially since it would be more limited than she had first feared. It might only be another half a beer.

Eighteen

It shouldn't take too much drinking, Immy figured, if she had really found the right place. She hoped she shouldn't have to go to more bars, but if she did, maybe it would be just parts of a few more light beers, if she had to stay long. Tex Mix was even smaller than Friendly's, which had had a longish bar and a row of booths. This outfit had a shorter bar top and only four freestanding tables with chairs. It would have fit inside Friendly's just fine.

There were fewer patrons, too. No women. Three sullen-looking older men, in cowboy hats, of course, huddled at the far end, leaving three empty stools. She took the one nearest the door and farthest from them. The bartender was a heavyset redheaded guy who had spent so much time in the sun that his freckles had nearly all run together across his face and down his arms.

"Whatcha need?" he asked, nicely enough.

"I'm so thirsty from my long ride. I just need a light beer before I head out again." She gave him the brand and her talk of travel got the ball rolling, as she'd hoped it would.

"Where y'all comin' from?" he asked as he popped open a can. Tex Mix apparently had no light beers on tap.

"Just down from Dallas, headin' for Slap Out."

"That's not all that long a drive."

She shrugged and batted her eyes. "I'm just not much used to driving distances. There's a story to cover in Slap Out."

"You a reporter then?"

Sure, since he brought it up. That would make as good a cover as any. "I am," she once again lied. "You hear about the murder there, on the day of a wedding?"

"Sure did. I knew the fella, too."

She opened her mouth and eyes with feigned surprise. "No way. You knew him?"

This had exactly the desired effect. He leaned his beefy freckled arm on the bar and lowered his head toward hers. "The guy that died in Slap Out was the one that knifed Claude Barrelson. Right here, in this bar." He tapped his sturdy finger twice on the bar top.

She expressed more incredulity. It was only party feigned. She was a little surprised and happy that she had the right place, after all. "Right here? Where exactly?"

With the same finger, he pointed to a spot on the floor about five feet inside the front door. "Claude was tryin' to get out the door, get away from him. They were all crazy drunk."

It was not a good idea to mention that he should not have let that happen. "So you saw it? You saw the whole thing?" This could not have been going better.

"Sure did. Claude was here with his girl, Alice May, and Junior was hittin' on her. Claude got in his face and Junior whipped out that knife. A big Bowie knife. He stuck him as he was tryin' to run out the door."

"Do you mind if I quote you in my article?" She fished her notepad and pen out of her purse and opened the notepad on the counter, pen ready to scribble.

"Don't mind at all. I'm Tex Kibbie, owner of this here bar."

He was probably the bouncer, too. If not, he should have been, and should have thrown them out before everything escalated. She wrote his name and a few words of what he'd said to jog her memory later. "This is terrific. Thanks so much. I'd better get going."

"There's a little more, if you want it. For the article. After Claude was down, Alice May socked one of them and got thrown on the floor. Then the other two started kickin' Claude on the floor. I came 'round the bar and broke that up. Threw 'em all out and called the cops."

She was writing while he talked. "Can you tell how exactly where he was stabbed?" She looked for a darkened area of the floor.

"Naw, not really. Lots of stuff happens in here. But it was right around there." He pointed again. To be sure, the floor was scuffed and stained, with blotches all over it. The thought of the "lots of stuff" made her want to leave quickly. At least before it got dark and filled up with the people who did "lots of stuff."

"Thanks for the great info. I have to be going."

She didn't run, but she made it to the van quickly. On her drive back to Slap Out, she kept picturing Long Hot Mike kicking a bleeding man while he was on the floor. And maybe throwing the woman, Alice May, out of the way. Looks sure weren't everything.

Thinking of Long Hot Mike seemed to conjure him up, since her phone rang with his number as she was pulling into the town. Should she answer it? She needed info, so yes, she should.

"Hi Long. How's it going?"

"Hey, not bad. Wondered if you want lunch."

She glanced at the dash clock. It was about 2 by now. "It's a little late." Should she go out with him again?

"I know. I got caught up in stuff. Just a snack?"

Maybe she could get his version of the bar fight. And see if he knew the family of Claude Barrelson. "Well, I haven't eaten either. So, sure. I'm in the car. Where do you want to meet?"

There wasn't much choice, but he named one she hadn't noticed. "Gordo's Tacos?" He gave her directions, telling her it was tucked behind the bank. Sure enough, as soon as she got back to Slap Out, she drove around the bank building and the small blue and green building appeared in its shadow.

She had remembered to stop at a filling station on the way so she could remove her disguise and become plain old Immy again.

Everything she'd used went into the bags from the store. An urge to want to return them popped up, but that would be impractical, since she had left that town. Anyway, she could use the disguise some other time, now that she would be handling Cases on a regular basis. Ideally.

When she entered the steamy, fragrant atmosphere of Gordo's, she spotted Long in the far corner with a platter of nachos already on the table. He looked as good to eat as the nachos.

"Hi," she greeted him. "I thought we'd be gone back home today, but we've decided to stay for a few more."

"That's great." He gave that killer smile. Now that she was with him, under his spell, it was hard to picture him shoving women to the ground and brawling in a bar. She studied the menu, wondering why he wanted to get to know someone who wouldn't be here much longer. He answered that one right away.

"You know, I'm thinking of moving. I was wondering if you could give me any pointers."

"On where to move?" Huh?

"I know where I want to move to. Wymee Falls. You're from around there, right? Junior was talking about the cousin, your mom."

She admitted that she was.

"I just want to know more about the town. I'd like to expand my business."

"The catering? Or the goats?"

"Oh, catering, not the goats. That just happened kind of by accident as a sideline. I'm probably getting rid of the goats. The opportunities for catering are, well, limited in this place. I think I do a pretty good job and I'd like to set up somewhere else. Somewhere better. What do you think of that idea?"

One little part of her rebel heart started a fast beat at the thought of this gorgeous man being near her a lot. The rational part kept the beat only moderately fast. "I'm not sure what I can tell you. What do you want to know?" After all, he could look up the population and figure out that he would have a lot more business there. Maybe she could work in an interview, an examination, here. On her Case.

"You know, Hillstown is a good-sized place. That might be a place to try first. It's closer to here."

He frowned. "Hillstown."

"Yes, do you know much about it? Do you go there very often?"

"I don't think that would work."

"Why not?"

"There was…some trouble there. That damn Junior ruined that town for me."

That damn Junior? Had he not liked him? Not been buddies with him? "How did that happen?" Was he actually going to talk about this right now?

"He got into a lot of trouble there."

"How did that ruin it for you?"

He looked away. "I was with him. Me and Wyatt were with him last time he got in trouble."

"When he stabbed Claude Barrelson?"

He jerked his attention back to her face. "You know about that?"

This was working. "He just died, so yes, it's in the news. What exactly happened that night? Did you stab him, too?"

"No! Jesus, no! Claude was with this really hot girl. She was kind of flirting with me, and Claude gave me a look, so I backed off. Then Junior went after her, but he didn't back off. Claude swung first. He started it."

Junior was the bad guy and Long was the good one? "So Claude had a knife too?"

"No." Long shook his head. "Junior didn't fight fair."

"He murdered the guy."

"I know, I know. He shouldn't have used the knife. And now that the guy died, I've had three gigs cancelled. Everybody knows I was there that night. Junior kind of ruined my life. I mean, I was getting gigs cancelled before that, just because of the scuffle, but now the guy's dead. No one will hire me here."

So that was the real reason he wanted to relocate. Everyone in this town seemed to be worried about how the death of a person would personally affect them. No one said they were sorry the guy died, sorry for him, sorry for his family.

After having gotten into the subject, Long was spitting mad. In fact, a few drops of spit flew onto the nachos. That was a shame. They were awfully good. She had only had two chips and the cheese was just right, melty, velvety. Could she say she wasn't hungry and leave now?

As she was formulating the announcement of her escape, Long was continuing. "I can't tell you how much I hate Junior right now. He's ruined my life." His beautiful eyes were hard, not beautiful at all, in this moment. And he did not like Ned Junior, that was clear.

"He kind of ruined his, too. And Claude's." She so wanted to point out how theirs were much more ruined than his. But she didn't. "You're alive."

"Huh. What kind of life? You're probably the only person in this town who will have lunch with me."

Was that true? Then maybe she shouldn't be doing that, either. Everyone else knew him better than she did. She looked around for the server, who was leaning on the counter, thumbing through her phone. How had he gotten the nachos? She didn't think she was going to get tacos. Or even a drink. Her phone was positioned conveniently beside her plate. She had done that in case she wanted to record something he said. Now she glanced at it.

"Oh my gosh, look at the time. I need to get going."

"You just got here. You haven't even ordered yet." He looked over at the phone enthusiast in the Gordo's shirt. "Hey, can we get some service over here?"

She took her time raising her head. "In a minute. I have to finish some things first."

Immy put her phone into her purse, but before she could get up, he grabbed her wrist. Hard.

"Ow, that hurts!" She jerked her hand out of his grasp. "Leave me alone. I have to go."

She could feel those eyes burning into her back as she walked out.

Driving to the Henrys' house, she was picturing Long Hot Mike knocking a woman to the ground. Yeah, he could do that. He was totally capable of it. He had just shown her that.

Nineteen

As Immy drove up, she saw a car departing. Her mother was in the driveway.

"Did you just get out of that car?" Immy asked.

"Yes, I certainly did. My cousin, Ouida, had communicated with me and had indicated that she would like my company for an unspecified amount of time. Therefore, she came here and picked me up to take me to her domicile."

"Why did she do that?"

"I surmised, and I think that assumption was confirmed by the visit, that she desired to converse with someone about her woes."

"Oh, poor woman. She does have woes."

"More than you can imagine."

"Well, I can imagine a lot. Her son has just been murdered."

"There are also issues with her spouse. He is not the ideal partner."

"I think you knew that, right?"

"Correct. The visit has left me with a degree of agitation. I am worried about her."

Immy gave her mother a hug. There probably wasn't much they could do for her. Besides maybe finding her son's killer.

After a quiet moment, they went inside, then found everyone in the backyard watching the little goat springing up and down and running in circles, throwing his head back and expressing himself in goat-speak.

Or maybe goat-bleat. Everything seemed to amuse and excite the adorable little guy. He would spring straight up for no reason at all, that Immy could see.

"Can we get one, Mommy?" Drew was panting, breathless from running around with Babalu. "He's so much fun!"

Immy smiled at the two of them. "Do you think Marshmallow would like him?"

"Marshmallow?" Lulu said. "You have to be careful with Long Tuttle's goats. They're not all this nice. The one that killed our little Ricky Junior would probably kill a pet named Marshmallow, too."

Immy stared at Lulu. "A goat killed one of your dogs?"

"Yes." Lulu's voice held a sob. "Little Ricky. Ricky Junior. He was Luci's pup. She had a litter and we sold all but one and kept Little Ricky. He was just a baby."

"We probably shouldn't have taken him over there," Victor said.

"Where?" Immy asked. The sulfur seemed very strong in the yard right now, even without a breeze. In fact, it felt like she was at the entrance to hell. Wasn't it supposed to be filled with sulfur? Fire and brimstone. She'd always thought that's what they smelled like. For some reason, she pictured Victor with devil's horns on his head. Why did she do that? He seemed like a nice man.

"To his goat farm," Lulu answered. "He was having a fair, he called it. I think he wanted to advertise that he was renting out goats for poison ivy."

"What do you mean?" Immy didn't get the connection.

"They love to eat poison ivy, so Long rents them out to people who have poison ivy problems. There's a ton of it in that oil field." She pointed to the pumps just behind their house. Immy remembered seeing some there where she found the feather.

"I have heard that said about bovids," Hortense said. "They are rapacious eaters."

"What happened to your puppy?" Immy asked.

"One of the biggest goats butted him so hard, he died." Now Lulu was openly sobbing. "Sorry. I have to go inside."

Immy looked at Victor. "Then why did you get another goat?"

"This one's a miniature. Long said he wouldn't hurt our dogs. The ones we have left are grown-up, much larger. He gave us Babalu to make up for Little Ricky. He owed us at least that much."

"Did he pay the vet bills?"

"He did, but that's just money. That little pup was a piece of Lulu's heart."

As much as they loved these adult dogs, Immy could imagine how much she would dote on a puppy. Victor, she would guess, was just as broken up about it, but, being a guy, didn't allow anyone to see that. No tears, but he swallowed loudly a couple of times. This little guy, Babalu, wasn't big enough to cause any harm to these dogs. Besides, they all got along and frolicked together. With Drew joining in.

"I believe I will retire to the interior of the abode before mosquitoes begin ravaging out here." Hortense made her way up the stairs and disappeared inside.

Victor offered to bring beer or iced tea out to everyone, and the adults settled on the porch steps to chat. Lulu, who had quit crying, came out to join them. She told Immy she had given some lemonade to Hortense in the kitchen.

After only a few moments, Immy sensed a lack of movement, noise, activity. She scanned the yard in the growing darkness and couldn't see Drew.

"Drew! Drew!" There was no answer. "Did any of you see where she went?"

"I suppose she's inside." Lulu wasn't being helpful. There's no way she could have gotten past them, up the porch steps, without someone noticing, without someone moving aside so she could get through.

Hortense had heard Immy call for Drew and had come outside. She stood on the porch, at the top of the steps and surveyed the yard. "The bovid ruminant seems to be absent also," Hortense helpfully added.

"Babalu is gone, too?" Immy set her beer can on the ground and ran around the yard for a few seconds before bolting out the back gate.

She could hear others following her, between her frantic shouts. They began calling Drew's name in a panicky chorus, the volume increasing as they all ran toward the pumps.

"Mommy?" Her voice was so small.

"Drew, baby! What are you doing here?" Immy scooped her up. She was glad to notice that the little goat was right there with them.

Lulu caught up to them, breathing heavily, and grabbed Babalu's collar. "What happened? Why did you go out here, Drew?" She seemed pretty worried about the child. Immy was touched.

"I thought I heard some people."

Immy tried to put some sternness into her words. "You absolutely must tell us whenever you go somewhere."

"Anywhere? To the baffroom?"

"Anywhere out of the house. Don't ever do that again, okay? What if the little goat had run away?"

"He wanted to go wiff me. He wasn't running away."

That seemed to be true. Even before Lulu took hold of his collar, he had been trotting alongside Drew.

"Okay, let's all go in the house now." Immy set her daughter down. She wasn't as light as she used to be, and she was growing every day, it seemed like. Then she dusted off her clothing. The child wasn't clean.

"Babalu in the house, too?"

"No, Drew, we'll go in, everyone except him."

They all walked back to the yard where Hortense waited at the gate.

"I'm greatly relieved to see all of you," she said.

In the yard, Immy could see better with the outside light on the porch. Drew was coated in goat hair, dog hair, and dirt, so Immy told her she needed a bath now.

"I'll do it, Imogene," Hortense said.

Immy followed them inside and saw the fruits of her mother's labors today on the countertop. Three pies sat cooling.

"Look at what your mother did." Lulu had come inside, too, and beamed at the pies. "She talked me through the apple one and I think I can duplicate it."

"Hers are awfully good."

"Where were you all afternoon? I thought you were going to be back for lunch."

"I meant to be, but I got delayed."

"Have you eaten?" Lulu listed some choices and Immy chose a cheese sandwich. "It's awfully nice of you to feed us. We should get out of your hair soon."

Lulu sat across the table from her and leaned close. "I've heard some rumors about you."

Immy was startled. What would the people in this town know about her? Rumor things, that is.

"I hear Eccles hired you as a detective. Is that true?" Lulu sounded impressed, not upset.

Ah, not really a rumor. "Well, yes, he did. I just got my private detective license. I'm going to try to find out exactly what happened to Ned Newberry, Jr."

"I can tell you one thing. There was some evidence there that points to someone."

"Something you found?"

"No, something the cops have. My nephew is a policeman in Ant Bite, a little town down the road, and they're helping with the murder." She leaned even closer. Immy picked up her sandwich and moved it aside a little. She didn't want spittle on all of her food today. "Guess what he was tied with, up there?"

"Rope?"

Lulu shook her head. "No, bungee cords. And not just any bungee cords."

Immy had picked up the sandwich and had been aiming it at her mouth, but stopped, midair. "Bungee cords," she repeated.

"Yes, guess what they said on them?"

She did better at answering this question. "Long Catering?"

Lulu nodded slowly and knowingly. Immy decided not to tell her who she'd been with earlier in the day. Lulu might learn about it through the Slap Out grapevine anyway.

How was she going to eat the rest of the sandwich with this sick feeling in her stomach? She remembered Lulu picking up a bungee that he'd left behind after the rehearsal dinner. At the time Immy had noticed it belonged to Long's catering business.

"Do they, does your nephew think Long killed Ned Junior?"

"I'm not sure. I don't know why they haven't hauled him in yet, though. Maybe they found more evidence. For someone else, I mean. Isn't Loryetta's daddy still in jail?"

Immy choked down a few more bites. "Can I save this for later? I just remembered someone I have to call."

"Sure, no problem." Lulu bustled around the kitchen, getting some wrap and putting Immy's sandwich in the cute little round-topped fridge.

Since Victor was still in the backyard, Immy stepped out the front door to call Long. A few thoughts were whirling around in her head. What if he was the killer? And she had just been with him. Had been seen with him. If he was, what did this mean to her Case? She hadn't even properly named it yet. Was it over already? Would she get paid for any of her legwork?

Before she could start calling Long, a call from Ralph came through.

"Hey Immy, do you know what you're doing? I mean when you're coming home? I just got the news at the station."

"News?"

"Yeah, about the dead guy."

"Ralph, he died two days ago." She started walking around the front yard, going toward the street so no one would hear them. "Why are your people just hearing about it now?"

"Not that one. The other one. The other dead guy."

"Ralph, what are you talking about? Another one? I haven't heard of anyone else dying." She felt her insides sinking.

"Immy, I'm coming up there. I don't want you there alone."

"I'm not alone. I'm in a houseful of people and dogs. And a goat."

"There's a goat in the house?"

She twirled back toward the house. "Not in the house. In the backyard. Ralph, I should go inside and help Mother with Drew's bath."

"I'll be there tomorrow. Chief said I could take a few days off."

"Ralph, I have to go."

"You're not gonna say you'll be glad to see me?"

She pretended she hadn't heard that last part and disconnected the call. She didn't have to go inside, though. She had to call Long. And she had to see who else had died.

But she didn't get an answer when she tried to call him. It rang immediately to his voice mail. She tried three more times, but had no luck. Frustrated, she stomped into the house. The TV was on and Lulu and Victor were both watching intently, eyes wide open.

"What's—"

They shushed her and she sat down to watch.

Twenty

The television was blaring out a report of a dead body found in an oil field just minutes before. It seemed to be near where Ned Newberry, Jr., had been discovered. This was Ralph's new dead body? She imagined she could smell sulfur right here in the house. That must be from just thinking about the oil field.

Or maybe from the excursion they had all made, looking for Drew. A chill ran down her spine, thinking about Drew out there. Had she heard the murder taking place? Or maybe just heard it being discovered? At least she hadn't come upon a dead body herself.

"The name is being withheld pending positive identification. The discovery was made today, shortly before this broadcast."

Immy ran out back to see if she could maybe tell what was going on in that oil field, so close to the Henrys' backyard. It had grown dark enough that she could see lights contrasting with the shadows. She went through the gate in the back fence and tried to sneak up to the scene. There were lights in the distance, but farther away than the pump where Ned Junior had been found. Was this commotion the place where the body had been found "minutes before" the broadcast? She had to find out.

She made her way toward whatever was going on, making out the shapes of cars and an ambulance as she drew closer. There was a road into the section of the oilfield where they were. Still, they had to have approached without sirens or she would have heard them from the house. They all would have, even from the inside.

Now she was almost there. The lights at the crime scene didn't illuminate the ground where she was. In fact the contrast made the dark darker, so she stumbled forward, trodding on plants and uneven ground, but managed to remain mostly upright. At one point she stubbed her toe on a rock, or clump of soil, or something—she couldn't see what it was—and she put her hand down on the ground, on some sort of plant, to catch herself. At least it wasn't prickly.

Stopping just short of the circle of light being cast onto the dirt, she stood still to hear the chatter. She could only make out snatches.

"—any more evidence bags? I need a couple over here."

"What do you think? He's still warm enough that…"

"I think we'd better get him to the M.E. pretty damn soon."

"Careful getting him off that fence. There might be—"

"Did you get the—"

"Where's the—"

"What are you doing here?" This was spoken by a tall man who had come up next to her without her noticing it. He wore a Slap Out police uniform. He told her to follow him and led her inside the circle of light, but not very near to the place where she saw a body bag being lifted onto a gurney.

"Who died?" she asked.

"We're not releasing that. Who are you? Where did you come from?"

"I don't live here. I'm visiting the Henrys. They live right over—"

"I know where they live. You're the one in from Saltlick for the wedding, aren't you? A cousin or something?"

"I'm Imogene. My mother is Hortense, the cousin of the mother of the groom, Ned Junior, the one who was found dead right around here."

He turned and shouted to the others. "She's right here. This is her."

Her? Oh no! What did he think she had done?

Another man walked over to her, his wrinkled face craggy in the half light. "I'm Chief Crane. You need to answer some questions. Powell, can you take her to the station?"

"Station?" Immy blurted out. "Why would I go to the station? I just wanted to see what was going on. I'll have you know that I've been hired to investigate the murder that happened here the other day."

"Come with me," said the first uniformed man, the tall one, who must have been Officer Powell.

"I need a lawyer. I'm not going anywhere." She planted her feet and folded her arms in defiance. She knew her rights. Or was pretty sure she did. "You can ask me questions here."

"Without a lawyer?"

"I don't need a lawyer. I haven't done anything wrong. What do you want to know? I had nothing to do with whatever happened here. I just walked over from the house."

"Is your name Imogene?"

"I said it was. Imogene Duckworthy." They didn't retain info very well. She got out her driver's license and showed it to him.

He nodded. "How do you know Long Tuttle?"

"Long Tuttle?"

"Yes, that's what I said."

"What's he got to do with anything?" Was he the killer, after all? Did they know she'd been with him earlier? "I just ran into him today at Gordo's. We had lunch."

"Why have you been calling him?"

"It's…it's about something he said earlier today." Not really, but they didn't know what they'd talked about. She thought fast. "My daughter wants to buy a goat from him." True, although she doubted she would do that.

"You've been calling him a lot."

How did he know that? Why were they asking about Long? The ambulance doors slammed shut and it took off, carrying the body bag with it.

"He wasn't answering. And why shouldn't I call him?" A horrible thought overcame her. The hairs on her arms and the ones on the back of her neck raised up, stiff. "Is that him? Is that Long? Is Long dead?" Her knees buckled and she stumbled forward.

"Ma'am, do you need to sit down?"

Yes, she did. When she opened her mouth, no words came out, so she nodded.

He gently took her arm and guided her to a police car, opening the back door and letting her sit there sideways with her feet out. No way was she going to get all the way in. No way was she going to the police station. Swallowing, with a huge and audible effort, she found her voice. "What's going on? What do you want to know?"

"I want to know why you were calling Long Tuttle."

"Is he the dead body or did he kill the dead body?"

"Never mind, just answer my question."

"But I did. I kept calling because I couldn't understand why he wasn't answering. I had just had lunch with him a couple of hours ago. I think it was around two or three. At Gordo's. Ask them. They'll tell you we were there."

"How do you know him?"

"I told you. Goats. And the wedding. That's where I met him. Then he was here about the goat he had brought for Lulu and Victor. I guess that was Saturday afternoon. The day the wedding was supposed to be. They named it Babalu and my daughter, Drew, loves it. She wants to get one from him. From Long Tuttle. But I don't know if he has any more of the little tiny ones like that. I don't think we should get a big one. After all, we already have a pet pig." She knew she was babbling, but she couldn't stop, even though her teeth wanted to chatter.

Officer Powell stopped her, though, for which she was grateful. "Okay, that's probably enough for now. We'll let you know if we need more information." He had written some things in a notebook, but it couldn't have been everything she'd said.

"Do you want my phone number?"

"We have it."

Oh no. Why was that? They must have gotten it from Long's phone. They had his phone. Of course they did. They knew she'd been calling him. That meant he was the person who was dead. Either that, or it meant they had taken it from him. Or that he had lost his phone out here. That wasn't very likely, though.

She trudged back through the dark, barren land to the Henrys' back gate. When she went inside the house, her mother and Lulu were putting dinner on the table. She sat like a zombie and ate without tasting anything. It might have been fried chicken, but it might have been tofu, unlikely as that was here.

She wasn't one hundred percent certain that Long Tuttle, Long Hot Mike, was dead, but she was over ninety percent. That meant he probably didn't kill Junior. Unless he did and someone knew it and killed him for killing Junior. That would be complicated. Her stomach hurt and her head started hurting too.

She ran to the bathroom to throw up. Kneeling on the floor in front of the porcelain throne, the palm of her right hand started burning, itching. Her hand had red angry bumps all over it and it felt like it was on fire.

After she wiped her mouth and cleaned everything up—she felt a lot better now—she showed her hand to her mother.

Lulu peered at it, too. "That's poison ivy. Where did you get into that?" Lulu rummaged in a cupboard and produced some calamine lotion and a plastic bottle of Benadryl. "Here, take this, and rub some of this on your hand. You'll have to redo it, but it should make you feel better."

Immy frowned, trying to think why she should have a poison ivy rash on her hand. Then she remembered stumbling in the dark just now and catching herself, touching a plant on the ground. She also remembered hearing them talk the other day about there being poison ivy around the oil pumps. After she slathered the thick, chalky stuff on her hand, she swallowed the pill.

Very soon, she started feeling a little dizzy. She needed to call Loryetta and find out what her status was. If she still had a Case, she needed to name it. The lotion was soothing, but the pill was making her sleepy. She needed to call her before she conked out.

Lulu had a bit more advice. "Try not to touch anything with that hand. You can spread it all over if you do."

It was her right hand. That was going to be hard.

She would also have to ask Drew what she had heard that led her out of the yard, and what had she seen, if anything.

Twenty-One

Her eyes were closing, hard as she might try to keep them open. Immy couldn't call Loryetta right now. She lay down to sleep, but the pill was affecting her mind. When she had been at the crime scene, had she heard them say they had to get Long off the fence? Why would a dead person be on a fence? Anyway, most of the fences around here were electric wire fences. You couldn't climb those, or even sit on them. Her mind was slogging through mud. It took a long time for her to drift off, picturing Long Tuttle, that gorgeous, deeply flawed man, climbing a ladder and tying Ned Junior to the walking beam. His words at their lunch echoed in her mind.

Junior kind of ruined my life.

She pictured him shoving women to the ground and kicking them, then frothing at the mouth while he talked about Junior, and getting his spit on her lunch.

The next thing she knew, Drew was shaking her shoulder. "Come on, you have to get a pancake before they're all gone."

Just before she ran her hands over her face, she remembered the rash on her palm. Then, fully awake, she was aware of how much it burned and itched. What if she had rubbed her eyes? But she had been able to sleep. The poison ivy hadn't kept her awake.

"I need some calamine lotion," she told Drew, jumping out of bed and hurrying to the bathroom to rub more of the soothing stuff on her hand.

"Cal-mine lotion?" Drew had followed her. "Can you eat that? Are you putting it on your pancake? It looks like stwawbewwy syrup."

Immy had to smile. "No, silly, it's not strawberry syrup. It's medicine to make my hand feel better." She shook the bottle, then tipped it carefully and poured some of the lotion onto her painful palm. "Drew, what did you hear, that made you want to go outside of the yard last night?"

"Just some people. I couldn't tell what they were saying, so I wanted to get close so I could hear the words, but I couldn't hear any."

"Did you see anything?"

"Lots of lights. I didn't get close enough to see any people. I think they were all men. I didn't hear any women."

"Okay. Thanks for telling me. You won't do that again, right?"

"Did you know that Unca Ralph is going to be here today?"

She stopped rubbing the lotion. "Today? He's coming here today?" She hadn't expected him to really do that. Yes, he said he was going to, but…

"Come on! Get your pancake! They might give it to Babalu."

At the table, Immy realized how hungry she was. She hadn't eaten much the day before. Everyone else had already finished by the time she got there and some lukewarm pancakes, which were still delicious, fluffy and light, were on a platter.

"Lulu, these are fantastic," she said, carrying a buttered and syruped forkful to her mouth.

"Oh, your mother made those," Lulu said from the sink where she was washing everyone else's dishes.

Victor was rummaging in the refrigerator. He pulled out a soda and added, "Lulu's will sit like a rock in your stomach. Your ma sure can cook."

Immy didn't miss the dark look Lulu shot him over the "rock in your stomach" comment. Trying to soothe it over, Immy said, "Oh, I'm sure that isn't true. My mother is a lot older than Lulu. She's been cooking for a long, long time."

Just then Hortense came into the kitchen from the living-dining room. "Who's been doing what a long, long time?"

"I was just saying what a good cook you are, and you've been cooking forever."

"My whole life. Not my entire existence, of course. Not when I was an infant, but for the part of my existence wherein I was old enough to do so. What should we make for Ralph?"

Immy didn't miss the look that passed between Lulu and Victor. "We can't have more people staying here," Immy said. "He'll have to go to the Motel Four."

"Oh my. He can't stay there." Hortense looked horrified. She rested her chubby hand on her ample bosom.

"Well, he shouldn't come here."

"It's rather late to render that judgment. I surmise he is halfway to Slap Out by now."

Immy groaned. Ralph was going to be in the house with them. "Oh no. I have a lot to do." She finished up her flapjacks and went into the backyard to phone Loryetta. "Do you have any news for me?" she asked.

"Yes, I'm so glad you called. Daddy has been released on bail and wants to see you right away."

The poor woman, trying to clear her own father of killing her own groom, discovered dead on a pumpjack.

It came to her then. She knew what her case was called, now that it was a Case. The Case of the Pumpjack Groom. That way she would always remember it. She would probably never have another case involving a pumpjack and a groom. Had they let Eccles Justice go because they thought Long Tuttle had killed Junior? If so, they would have to find Long's killer now.

Driving to the Justice house, following the directions Loryetta had given her, an awful thought sprang up. Had Eccles maybe killed Long? She would have to find out when he had been released so she could tell whether or not he could have done it. This was an awfully complicated case for her first official one. More dead bodies than she would have liked. She had to do a good job here so she would get recommendations from these people. If she found that her client was actually guilty, that would not be good. Then she wouldn't use this case, of course, and she would have no referrals. And no record.

*****

The house, a grand old Victorian with a wraparound porch and a soaring tower, stood proudly and sedately on a corner, kept company by other grand old houses along the street. Immy parked the van at the curb and walked up the porch steps. The front door was inset with an etched oval of glass, but there was a doorbell, so she didn't have to rap on the delicate-looking window. The wooden part of the door looked so thick she doubted it would make a noise inside if she knocked on it.

A woman Immy didn't recognize answered the door.

"Yes?" she said, not recognizing Immy either.

"Hi, I'm Immy Duckworthy, Hortense's daughter? Loryetta told me to come over?"

"Oh! I thought she said a private investigator was coming."

"Yes," Immy said, with a proud smile. "That's me."

"I had no idea it would be someone like you." Did she like the idea or not? Immy couldn't tell.

"Is she here? Is Mr. Justice here?"

"We're both here." Loryetta appeared behind the woman, who may have been a housekeeper, much to Immy's relief. She hadn't been sure she would get past the woman to do her job. Immy followed the bereft bride into a lavish living room, full of ornate, uncomfortable Victorian furniture sitting with their scrolled legs sunken into a deep, plush Oriental carpet. She waded through it to get to the brocade settee where Mr. Justice sat, nursing something dark-colored and strong-smelling in a crystal glass.

"Hi, I'm—"

He stopped her. "I remember you from the rehearsal dinner. Please, have a seat."

She perched opposite him on a long sofa with a hard brocade seat and Loryetta sat at the other end of it.

"Do you mind if I take notes?" She thought it would look professional to do that, and she had a pad of paper and pencil in her purse.

"I hope you do," he answered. "What do you need to know?"

What *did* she need to know? "I need information to clear you of Ned Newberry, Jr's murder. So, can you tell me where you were at the time?"

"Do you know when he was killed?"

"He was wearing his tux for the wedding, so it would have to be Saturday morning. Do you have a good alibi for the whole morning?"

"I thought you were going to find out who did this, not interrogate me."

Good grief. Was he going to be hard to work with? Impossible to work with? "I need to have information to clear you, first. That's your best defense. Then we can work on other suspects. I mean, work on suspects." She must stop thinking of him as a suspect. He was a client. Yes, a client. If a cranky one. "I think, though, that we should lay out our terms first."

Loryetta interrupted them. "I think Neddie took his clothes with him the night before. He told me he might stay in his car that night and he wanted to have everything with him."

So the groom had probably anticipated being too drunk to drive until morning. And also being hung over then.

"Do you have a contract?" Mr. Justice asked.

She was so glad that she did. "Yes, it's right in here." She dug it out of her purse and handed it to him. She had filled in the amounts, deposit, daily fee, and checked the box for extra expenses as needed. While he ran over the papers, she held her breath. After all, she didn't have a Case until she had a contract.

"This looks fine."

She tried not to look too relieved while he signed it. He even pulled some bills out of his wallet and paid her the deposit. She countersigned, gave him a receipt, then continued trying to get information to clear him. It wasn't easy.

"Who all saw you on Saturday morning?"

"I woke up fairly early." His steady stare was disconcerting. "We had breakfast, the family, then the maid and Loryetta went to the church to get her ready."

"So you were alone in the house then? For how long?"

"I showered and dressed after they left. I suppose it was an hour. Maybe longer. I don't know what time I got to the church."

There was a chance he would have had enough time. If he was a fast dresser. "Who saw you arrive?"

He shrugged, keeping that steady gaze. "I don't really remember. Maybe no one."

This wasn't going to be easy. Maybe he actually was the killer. And maybe Junior had been killed earlier than Saturday morning, since he might have dressed the night before. "Did you see Junior on Saturday, at all?"

"No, how could I? He was out there, dead, roped to that piece of metal."

That was a good sign, that he thought Junior was roped to the pump, since he hadn't been. It might even be a sign that he didn't do it.

"Can you remember who the first person you saw at the church was?"

He finally looked away, screwing up his eyes trying to remember. "I saw the reverend. No, I saw the organist before that. She was going into the sanctuary before anyone else to get the organ warmed up."

Immy made a note to talk to both of those people and see if they knew what time he'd gotten to the church.

"Now listen, little missy, the only reason I was put in jail was one piece of evidence they found at the scene. My cufflink was there. As soon as they interviewed enough people who told them I lost the damn thing at the church, they knew I was being framed."

Framed! "Oh, so the charges have been dropped?" Was her first Case going to vanish as soon as it got started? And what was with calling her "little missy"? That would not do. "You are free to call me Imogene. Or Ms. Duckworthy." She tried to match his glare.

He did look away. "No, they have not been dropped. But they don't have any evidence against me."

How did that work? Was he confused about what was going on?

"Okay, that's enough of that." His piercing gaze was back. "Now, let's talk about who did kill Ned Junior."

Twenty-Two

OKAY, SHE WAS WILLING TO LOOK FOR OTHER SUSPECTS. That was half of the reason she was here. Was someone scattershot placing evidence to frame others? Mr. Justice's cufflink and Long's bungie cords? She needed to know a lot more and hoped this man could tell her some of what she had to find out. "Did you know Junior well?" Immy asked.

"Of course he did." Loryetta turned to Immy. "Neddie was gonna marry me. My daddy knew who he was, even if we didn't grow up together."

"Where did he grow up?"

"Oh, he was mostly away. In boarding schools, you know," she said.

"They were able to give him a private education in his early years," Mr. Justice added. "Myself, I think the local schools do a fine job. The parents have good control of the school boards."

Immy bent her head and scribbled nonsense on her pad. Junior probably stopped being able to go to an expensive private school when his father was sent to prison. She wondered what Mr. Justice meant by controlling the school board. Did he want to control everyone and everything? Was he in control of who his daughter was marrying? "Who were Ned Junior's main associates?"

Mr. Justice answered first this time. "His two closest friends were Wyatt and Long."

She nodded. She already knew about those. "Any other friends? Or any enemies? People who really didn't like him?" Long maybe used to be a close friend, but he hadn't sounded like it when they had lunch together.

Mr. Justice shrugged, so Immy looked at Loryetta, but she shrugged, too.

"Well, somebody killed him. Somebody must have not liked him."

Loryetta spoke up. "It doesn't even make sense. A lot more people disliked his daddy."

"Now, Loryetta, darlin', don't go talkin' like that."

"Well, it's true, Daddy. You and Neddie's daddy have a lot of enemies around here."

Mr. Justice leaned forward, toward his daughter. He looked menacing, to Immy. "I said, don't go talkin' like that. You hear me?"

"Yes, Daddy." Loryetta sank back and hit the hard, unyielding pillow behind her. She reached around, grabbed it, and threw it onto the floor. The glare of Mr. Justice grew even more cold and threatening. She got up, replaced the pillow, and left the room.

Immy realized that she was pretty much at a dead end with this guy. But maybe there was one more thing to try. "Who do you think killed him? You, personally?"

The man actually tilted his face toward the ceiling and appeared to ponder her question. "I've been putting some thought into that. It couldn't be my partner, Ned Newberry—he's Neddie's daddy. You don't kill your own son. I would be surprised if it was one of the boys, Wyatt or Long. Maybe Wyatt's daddy? All I know is, it wasn't me."

"You mentioned being framed. Who would want to do that to you?"

He stared. "That, Ms. Duckworthy, is quite a long list."

He stood and she assumed this interview was over. "Will you please let me know if you think of anything or anyone else? Or if you see something or hear something."

"And what are you going to be doing?" That stare again.

No doubt the man wanted his money's worth. "I'll be going over the evidence. I might have another source."

He looked surprised. "Oh, might you, now? And who would that be?"

"I'm afraid I can't say." She hoped this would sound like she actually had a source and couldn't divulge the name, instead of actually not having one, but hoping to get one. She stood, glad to be off the uncomfortable couch. "Thank you for your time. I'll be reporting back to you with any new developments." Please, she thought, let there be new developments. Maybe Ralph could get her some information on the evidence. She already had some. She would have to ponder what she knew and what she needed to know.

The maid or housekeeper, or whatever, didn't make another appearance, nor did Loryetta, while she let herself out of the stuffy, ornate, uncomfortable house.

It was mid-morning on a Tuesday. Maybe the organist or the minister, or both, would be at the church. When she drove into the parking lot, there was a sedan and a pickup. Could she be this lucky?

She could. The full throaty tones of the pipe organ greeted her as soon as she opened the door. After sitting in a pew at the side of the sanctuary for only a few minutes, the organist noticed her. She turned toward Immy and tilted her head, questioning.

Immy ran to the railing around the altar area, where the console of the instrument was. "Excuse me, I'm investigating for Mr. Justice and I wonder if you could just help me out a little?"

The musician, a young, tall, slim woman, had very long fingers. Probably ideal for playing an organ, Immy thought. She walked down the half dozen carpeted steps, sort of gliding instead of taking actual steps. "Sure. What can I tell you?"

"Well, I need to know when Mr. Justice got to the church the morning of the wedding. For his alibi. The police have been questioning him."

"Oh goodness, he was here early. He came pretty soon after his daughter, and I'm pretty sure he stayed here the whole time. I can't imagine that Chief Crane would think Eccles would kill his daughter's groom."

"Oh, I'm sure they're questioning everyone. Thanks for the information."

In her car, making a note, she wondered what she thought she would learn here. Okay, he'd come early to the church. But, depending on when Ned Junior was killed, he could have done it before that. Like, really early in the morning. Or he could have left and come back without the organist noticing. But surely he would have gotten his clothes messed up.

She drove down the road a bit, then pulled into the parking lot of a pizza store. What did she know? She knew that a cufflink had been recovered, but it probably belonged to Eccles Justice, so she didn't want to consider that for evidence, him being her employer right now. She knew that the bungee cords used to tie the body to the metal beam were from Long's Catering. But would he have used his own belongings, clearly labeled, for this? Some of them had been left behind in the church and the killer could have picked them up to later incriminate Long. Was someone framing both of them?

Wait! Now Long had probably been killed, too. Was the killer an enemy of Long? Was Junior collateral damage, used to frame him? What if Long was the main target? If only she could find out whose fingerprints were on the bungee cords. Could you even leave fingerprints on them?

She felt like crying. What if she wasn't going to be able to solve this Case? Her first try at being an official PI, and she was going to be a failure. After sniffling for a minute or two, she straightened her shoulders and started driving again. Someone killed those men. That was her starting point. There had to be a way to figure this out. She would approach the problem using the last murder. Who wanted Long dead? If she found that out, she might solve both murders.

Ralph's white pickup was in the driveway when she got back to the Henrys'. Great. Just what she didn't need right now. She would keep her cool. She would not let him talk her into quitting. If he wanted to take Hortense and Drew back home, he could. He was not going to take her back.

"Immy, where have you been?" Lulu asked when she came through the front door.

Ralph was there, standing in front of Lulu and Victor. He must have just arrived. She should have felt his vehicle hood to see how warm it was. That's what a PI should do. Get evidence, not have to guess at stuff.

She decided she would tell her. She would tell everyone. This was something she was proud of. "I'm working on a case. I've been hired to investigate the murders."

"So your PI business is a going concern?" Lulu smiled. Was she happy for Immy, or was that a condescending smile?

"More like an ongoing concern." Ralph would have to make a snide remark.

Immy tried to give him the glare Mr. Justice had given her. Had Lulu started to laugh at Ralph's insult? "I've received a deposit and have a signed contract. Yes, it's a going concern."

Ralph looked surprised. "Sorry, I didn't know. Someone really hired you?"

"Yes, someone *really* hired me." She didn't say, "What are you gonna do about it?" But she wanted to. "What are you doing here?"

"I came to see what's going on."

"I've been telling you what's going on."

"You didn't tell me you had a contract."

Immy relented and gave him a smile. "It was just signed today. I haven't had a chance to tell you. Excuse me, I have to review my notes." She turned her back on him and headed to the guest bedroom, but he followed her.

"Immy, I'm so worried about you. Someone is killing people here. People who are connected to the wedding."

"That's not why they're being killed. The two men weren't killed because they were at the wedding. The groom never even made it there."

"Then why were they killed?"

That was the question. Maybe it would do her good to talk this out with him.

"That's my next step. Widen my pool of suspects."

"Who's in it now?"

She plopped down onto the bed, letting her breath out. "Well, I guess I don't really know that my client didn't do it."

"He hired you, right? Would he do that if he were guilty?"

"It was his daughter, mostly, who hired me. She talked him into it."

"Could she have done it?"

Immy thought about that. Loryetta had had reservations about marrying the guy. "She did tell me she didn't want to be hitched to him after he had a murder conviction."

"What? The groom murdered someone?"

Immy told Ralph about the bar fight and about Ned Junior attacking the guy who had died a few days ago. "The guy wasn't technically murdered until he died, and that was after Junior was killed. But Loryetta thought the guy might die, and if that happened, then she didn't want to marry Junior. Neddie, she calls him."

"So do you think she might have killed him?" He sat on the bed next to her, but apart.

"There are easier ways to get out of marrying someone. And I don't see how she could have. Everyone was with her, helping her to get dressed, doing her hair, getting her ready for the ceremony. Everything is so complicated. I guess we don't really know the time of death."

"Do you know what evidence there is?"

She told him about the evidence pointing to Eccles Justice and to the very most likely now deceased Long Tuttle. "It looks to me like somebody was trying to frame everyone."

"Well, maybe just two people. I agree, the bride probably didn't do it. Unless there are things we don't know. What else do you have? What else do you know about these people?"

It cheered her that he said "things *we* don't know." That meant he was getting into this. "That they're crooks. Both families, the ones of the groom and the bride. They swindled people out of oil rights when they sold them land. Oh, and that Loryetta is pregnant."

Ralph stood. "You're kidding. You really should not be here in this place. It's a hotbed…of something."

She got to her feet and faced him. "This is exactly where I need to be. I have a Case. It's the Case of the Pumpjack Groom."

He frowned. "Immy, that's a terrible name."

That made her mad. "You are not going to stand here and insult my Case. Get out of this room."

He took a couple of steps before she called him back. "Wait, don't go. I need you to help me. You need to tell me what the police know. Get all the evidence for me."

"I can't do that. How do you think I'm supposed to do that?"

"You can hang around with the Slap Out cops. Find out what they know."

He shook his head and walked out of the bedroom.

Twenty-Three

THIS WAS A SETBACK. When Ralph was on his way here, she was thinking he could maybe at least help her out. Maybe. Well, she thought he might. She thought she could talk him into it. Was he going to end up being more of a hindrance than a help?

When she finally left the bedroom, Ralph seemed to be waiting for her. "I think there might be someone you're overlooking."

"Who would that be?" Hadn't she interviewed everyone? Drew was in the backyard, so they could speak freely.

"Well, look. Two guys have been killed. They were all close friends with the other one, and he hasn't been killed."

That was true. She hadn't talked to the third one of the bar fighters, the only one left alive. "You're right. You know, there were three who were good friends with each other for a long time and hung out together, but Long was pretty mad at Junior after he went overboard at the Tex Mix."

"Tex Mix? What about it?" Lulu had just entered the living room from the kitchen and heard the last couple of words. "That's the place where Junior stabbed the guy, right? He must have been completely out of control that night. So drunk." She shook her head.

"Long told me that they were all out of control. Tex, the bartender told me that Long attacked a woman that night. And Long, himself, admitted to me that he did."

"When did you see Long?" she asked.

"I happened to run into him. And we talked." And almost had lunch, practically, almost, a date, but Ralph didn't need to know about that.

Victor had joined the group. "Do you really think Eccles didn't kill either of them? Oh wait, he was in jail when Long was killed."

"Not really," Immy answered. "He had gotten out. It kind of looks like someone is trying to frame Mr. Justice, Eccles, though. And Long Tuttle, too. Do either of you know who would want to frame Mr. Justice?"

Lulu and Victor looked at each other. She answered. "A lot of people don't like him. We didn't, but we mostly didn't like Ned Newberry, Junior's dad. Our little Davey—"

"Now, Lulu, that was a long time ago."

"What was a long time ago?" Immy asked, but didn't get an answer.

She had a direction now, though, thanks to her conversation with Ralph. She should interview the only one of the younger trio left alive, Wyatt Harbor. The two who were dead had been his good buddies. That disastrous bar fight must have changed everything for them. If Wyatt detested both of them as much as Long had seemed to detest Junior, maybe he killed both of them. Their relationship soured into something. Hatred, or something else? As far as she knew, nothing had been found at the scene of Long's murder, on the electric fence, that would frame anyone. But she had no way of knowing, since she didn't have access to the police information. And it didn't look like Ralph was going to help her out with that. It would be so simple for him to buddy up to the local cops and milk them for inside info. Why wouldn't he do that for her? It was infuriating. She would try to work on him.

To that purpose, she took a seat next to him on the couch. "So, how's your case going?"

"I told you, Immy, it's not that big a deal."

Hortense was listening. "What is transpiring in Saltlick while we are absent?"

"Someone robbed the library," Ralph said. "Immy didn't tell you?"

No, Immy hadn't told her. She didn't want her mother to worry about that. The library had been her home for many years and she would be upset about it.

"Good heavens! How many books were taken? Rare books?" Hortense clutched her chest. Immy hoped she wouldn't have a heart attack. That was why she had kept it from her.

"No, ma'am. Just some petty cash."

"Surely there was not an abundance of that on hand."

"Nope, not much at all. Five seventy-five."

"Five dollars? To what purpose was that crime carried out, then?"

"We don't rightly know. Still working on it."

"It hardly seems worth it." Hortense rose and glanced toward the kitchen. The library robber case was over and done with for her, as long as the books were still okay. "I have been remiss. I must take something to my cousin. There remains one of the pies we made the other day." Immy figured she had dismissed the library business.

Lulu followed her to the kitchen to help. They left soon in Lulu's car.

Immy still wanted to try to talk Ralph into helping her. She picked up his big, strong hand, holding it in hers and stroking his palm lightly.

That backfired a bit, though. Holding his hand felt so good, that other thoughts flew out of her head and her mind turned to trying to figure out how they could get into the same bedroom that night. She was almost glad when he pulled his mitt out of hers so her mind could clear.

"Okay." She stood and spoke to Victor and Ralph. "I have a job to do, so I'll see all of you later."

She walked out the front door with her purse, which contained her brand-new credentials and her notepad. Now she had to find out how to tackle an interview with Wyatt Harbor. She needed to know where he lived, first of all. Why hadn't she found that out? The Henrys certainly knew that. So did the Justices. From her car, before she started driving, she phoned Loryetta.

"Could you tell me where Wyatt Harbor lives?"

"Immy, do you think he killed them?"

"It's something I have to consider. But I need to talk to him, at least."

Loryetta was silent for a moment. "Can I come with you when you talk to him?"

Why would she want to do that? "I don't want this to be too complicated. I have my own interrogation techniques, so I'd better see him one on one."

After another silence, she gave Immy the address. His house was off the main road, tucked in with other smaller houses on a side street. The yard, from the driveway to the porch steps, was dirt, and some of it was muddy, but she managed to get across the yard without getting her shoes too dirty.

After she rapped on the front door, she didn't know what to expect. Wyatt? His mother? His father? A brother or sister? Wyatt himself answered the door. She remembered him clearly from the rehearsal dinner. He was the blond man who had sat beside his father. Now she recalled how he had been blushing that night whenever Loryetta got near him. Life was hard when you were that fair-skinned.

"Wyatt Harbor? I'm Imogene Duckworthy, private investigator, and I'd like to ask you just a couple of quick questions, if you don't mind?"

He frowned. "I remember you. What is this about? Are you a reporter?"

"No, definitely not. I'm a PI, just like I just said. I'm doing this for my job."

"Who are you working for?"

"I'm not at liberty to say." She wasn't sure that information was confidential, but maybe she could get further that way. "There are a few matters we'd like to clear up." She was proud that she sounded so official. And that it was working.

Still frowning, he held the door open for her to enter. He gestured toward a sagging brown sofa and sat himself in a purple velvet recliner. Immy's quick glance around the room showed her that nothing matched. None of the furniture seemed to have been bought to go with any of the rest of it. The arm of the brown couch had a visible layer of gray dust on it.

"Are your parents home?"

"My mother's dead. I don't know where my dad is. Is this about the murders?"

This town was hard on mothers. Loryetta didn't have one either. "Yes." She could tell him that much. "I didn't know about your mother. I'm so sorry for bringing that up."

He shrugged. "So, why are you here?"

"We're trying to pin down the whereabouts of everyone to see if someone saw something that would give us information."

"Whereabouts when?"

"Let's start at the rehearsal dinner."

There was that blush. It crept up from his neck and engulfed his cheeks.

He didn't answer, so she prompted him. "I saw you sitting next to your father until the three of you young men left together. Right?"

"Right!" He nodded his head so quickly, she thought she might be wrong. He might be hiding something.

"Where were you for the whole dinner? Were you at the table that whole time?"

"That's where I was. The whole time. That night, the whole time."

"And after that? The day of the wedding?"

"She told you?"

Okay, what was this? She nodded wisely. She hoped. "Can you tell me in your own words?"

"Nothing happened. I wanted to, but I couldn't get her to do it. What did she tell you? Did she tell you we had sex?"

Sex? With Loryetta? Immy was speechless. No wonder Loryetta had wanted to come with her. She probably wanted to warn him not to say what he had just said. Recovering her voice, she cleared her throat and started, "Well..."

"It was just a quickie. She was going to be married in a few minutes, really, so that was my last chance. And I just about had her talked into it, when they came in and told us about Junior."

She closed her mouth, which had fallen open, she realized. "The night before the wedding? You were somewhere else then?" Bending over her notebook, she made some scribbles to cover up her confusion.

"I saw her going into the bathroom alone at the rehearsal dinner, so I followed. She's been teasing me for months. Leading me on. She kept saying we would hook up before she got hitched. Well, I thought this night was the last minute, the last chance before she got hitched."

So Wyatt had been seducing the bride while the groom was being murdered. That let him off the hook. Her, too.

He looked ready to cry. "But she wouldn't do it. She wouldn't come through. Not that time."

"What do you mean, that time? There was another time?"

"She didn't tell you?"

Another sage nod. "I need it in your own words."

"In that room where she got dressed. There was a closet. We did it in there. Then they came and told us, like I said."

She was getting more intel than she thought she would. "Then you heard that Junior's body had been found."

He nodded. She actually wrote some of this in her notebook.

"What did you do after the three of you went out the night before, after the dinner?"

"I got awful drunk. I couldn't get hold of my dad to drive me home, so I walked. It wasn't far."

"You didn't have a car?"

"No, Long drove us all to the bar. I guess he drove Junior home. I didn't want to be with them anymore. Tell you the truth, I was getting tired of being with both of them. My dad told me I needed new friends. He always tells me that. Not that he has any social skills, but I kind of agreed with him."

She closed her notepad and rose. "Thank you for your time. This has been very helpful."

"Who all you talking to?"

"I'm afraid that's confidential."

"I didn't see anyone kill Junior or Long, just so you know."

"Okay. Thanks." She was a little unclear on the timing of everything he'd told her, but he didn't seem like he'd been concentrating on killing the groom.

There was something oppressive about that dreary house. Maybe it would look better if Wyatt's mother were alive to coordinate some of the furnishings. Or to vacuum them.

Twenty-Four

"Wait."

Imogene was halfway to Wyatt Harbor's front door.

"I need to know who you think did this." He had started across the small room after her.

"That's funny. I need to know who *you* think did it."

"Not sure. But it might have something to do with Junior's old man. Or Loryetta's. Or both of them."

She sighed and returned to the brown, saggy couch and got her notepad out again. "Why do you think that?"

"Well, you know all about what happened, right?" He stood before her, trying to decide where to put his hands.

Now what? She forgot to nod wisely and furrow her brow.

He retreated to the chair again. "I know, it's kind of hard to understand. All this legal stuff."

"Do you understand it?" Maybe this was the equivalent of a wise nod. "Can you explain it to me?" Or an ignorant nod.

"I'll try. See, these old geezers inherited huge ranches from their own daddies. And it was stolen land that they got. My mother's family, the Garcias, came to Texas from Mexico when they were given a land grant a long time ago, in the seventeen hundreds. They ranched around here for over a hundred years, then there was the revolution and Texas was a Republic for a few years."

Immy scribbled furiously, not wanting to tell him to slow down. These were things she didn't know anything about, not anything at all.

"But then Texas was made a state and the land that had always been owned by my family was stolen and given away in the early eighteen hundreds by Austin."

"Austin? Stephen F. Austin?"

"No, the capitol. That's where this was all done. See, me and my family didn't even know about any of this until my dad started digging around. Our family was squeezed into a small piece of land where we could only raise a few head of cattle."

"Can you appeal this somewhere?" This wasn't right.

"Nope. It's all official. All legal as shit. When Eccles and Ned decided they would start selling off some of their land, my dad bought some back. That's kinda what made him look into everything and find out the history from my mom and her family. It was our land he had to buy back. My mom had two old uncles living back then, but they're long dead now. It was right after that Mom got sick. Cancer. She knew the old family stories, but had never told them to my dad, until then. We're all that's left of her family now."

"So her family told him you'd been swindled out of your land?"

"Not really swindled. Like I said, it's all legal. Or we thought it was."

"I'm not understanding. So what did you mother tell you and your dad?"

"That the land once belonged to us. But there's more. Just before she died, she told him her family had always thought there was oil beneath our land. She told him he should drill for oil." Wyatt's face screwed up and it looked like he was going to cry.

"And did he?"

"Ha!" he sneered. "That's when he found out. Right after we buried her. He had paid good money for a thin layer of dry land, for topsoil. And the mineral rights didn't go with it."

"That's what that stuff at the dinner was all about?"

Wyatt's shoulders slumped. "Dad gets so upset every time someone mentions it. I wish he never knew about the old history. It makes him so mad, on top o' all this. And then Ned bragged about finding that new oil under the land my dad just bought. Right to his face."

"That must have made both of you awfully mad. Do you know what your dad did the rest of the night?"

"He went home and drank a lot."

She thought it was time to leave Wyatt. But she pulled over a few blocks from the Harbor house to finalize her notes on what Wyatt had told her. It looked pretty much like she could cross him off as a suspect, since he was having sex with the bride that morning. And trying to at the dinner the night before. His father had a great motive, but he seemed to have gone home and gotten drunk. She would see if she could check this with Loryetta. Delicately.

She had to cross off these two, unless she found out something more, to contradict what Wyatt had just told her.

Going over her notes in the car before she got out at the Henrys', she realized that Wyatt might have a very good motive, though. If he and Loryetta were hitting it off, and she thought she was making a mistake, would he be the one to fix the mistake? To clear the way for them to be together? He would be marrying into the family that had stolen his land. He could get it back. Loryetta might have even encouraged Wyatt. If he was the one who did it.

But Wyatt didn't seem like that kind of guy. Or did he? He ran around with the other two and they were both violent. Maybe they were all three violent.

Was she ever going to figure this out? Her clues, the ones she knew about, were a cufflink, bungee cords, and a feather. And maybe none of those were really clues to anything. They could have all been planted to frame others, and one of those others was now dead. Everyone had good reason to kill both of those men, from what she'd found out. No matter how good looking one of them was.

More information! That's what she needed! She really did need to find out what evidence the police had collected at the second murder site. It wasn't far from the first one. They had already collected the stuff there, but she had found that feather after they had left the first site. Maybe she should go back and check out the area around the fence. She would be careful not to touch it, since Long had gotten electrocuted on it. At least, that's what it had looked like.

She got out of the van and went into the Henrys' house. She must have opened the front door quietly, because Lulu and Victor were talking to each other, had their backs to the door, and didn't hear her come in. She caught a sentence from Victor.

"I had a damn good reason to kill the son of a bitch."

Immy stood quietly just inside the door, without closing it, to keep it from making a noise.

"Victor, we both could have, back then. I'm glad I didn't have to, anyway."

"Anyone who could steal a dog right from a person's yard."

"And there's Davey. But don't get so excited, dear."

A car honked outside on the street. Immy shoved the door wide open and spoke loudly. "Hi, I'm back." She hoped they wouldn't know she'd been eavesdropping.

But, had Victor killed one of them? Which one? Someone had stolen a dog from them? There might be a way she could figure this out. But a little later. Farther out from this conversation, so they wouldn't think that she'd been eavesdropping. That wasn't polite.

"Hi, Immy." Lulu turned to her with a smile. "I think Victor and I would like to have the evening to ourselves."

"Yes, I'm so sorry. We have outstayed our welcome. And it was so kind of you."

"No, no, that's not what I meant. I mean we're going to go out together. We usually have a date night on the weekend, but this last weekend—well, it just wasn't possible. We'll be at Gordo's. If you want to go out, feel free. Or you can stay in and cook."

Which Immy knew meant that Hortense would cook. "Oh, how nice. What a great habit to get into. Don't worry about us. We'll figure something out."

"Your mother and daughter, and Ralph, went to the park. They should be back soon."

"Okay, thanks. I wondered where they were." Ralph's truck was missing, come to think of it, but she had been too deep in thought, looking at her notes and pondering her Case, to even notice that.

She wanted to talk to her mother about the visit to her cousin, Ouida Newberry. Maybe she could have asked Lulu, but she didn't get the chance.

Victor and Lulu were gone within a few minutes and Immy had the house, and the animals to herself. She should probably try to locate her family, but decided to go over her notes some more instead. She also needed to formulate an approach for finding out about a stolen dog.

Twenty-Five

Now what? She'd gone over and over everything. One minute she was sure Wyatt must have killed them both. The next, that Long killed Junior and…someone killed him. Junior's dad? Or did Eccles kill all of them? Or Sydney, Wyatt's dad?

No one had returned to the Henrys' house yet and she hadn't gotten any texts. It was still light enough that she could maneuver her way through the oil field to that electric fence without, she hoped, mishap.

On her way to the back door, she peeked into Lulu and Victor's bedroom. The dresser was full of pictures of their dogs. Maybe there would be a picture of the one someone had stolen? She tiptoed in, hoping her family, or worse, Lulu or Victor, wouldn't return right then and catch her.

There were quite a few frames that held the four dogs, together and separately, and a few that included little Ricky, who had died. She could tell because he was a puppy. Behind those, though, there were a few more. She stood on tiptoe to see them. Two of them included a lovely black poodle, miniature-sized. Was that the dog that had gotten stolen?

She knew the picture of the little boy was in another drawer. Was he Davey, the person Lulu had mentioned a couple of times? Victor had cut her off every time she did.

She left the room without having touched anything.

Being careful to shut all the animals into the backyard, she left through the rear gate and made her way to where she thought she remembered that Long had been killed. It was disappointing. The ground was completely trampled. There were no feathers or cufflinks, or bungee cords.

There must be something, she told herself, and scoured the area, walking slowly and keeping her head down to look for clues in the dirt. There was plenty of light, so she should be able to see something, if anything was there. She walked alongside the fence, being careful not to touch it.

However, she missed seeing a bump in the ground and stumbled. Against the fence! Her shoulder hit the wire and stung like a bee had gotten her. She had to push herself off with her hands, and that stung again. But none of them were very bad stings. Not even as bad as a wasp sting.

"Huh," she said to herself, rubbing her arm and her hands. That wasn't enough of a shock to kill anyone. It made sense, when she thought about it. Farmers wouldn't want their livestock to die on a fence, just to avoid it, and not plow through it.

So this fence had not killed Long. She started walking the length of the fence, looking for clues on the wires themselves. When she came to the place she remembered, where Long's body had been, as near as she could tell, and where there were the most footprints, there was some fabric caught on the fence, where the wire twisted together at the post. She asked herself, what had he been wearing? Blue jeans. That's what most people always wore here, no matter how hot it was. Just like at home in Saltlick. She squeezed her eyes closed to remember him in the diner. He had on a green plaid shirt, short-sleeved, when they met there earlier in the day.

Opening her eyes, she peered at the fabric. It was a tiny piece, but part of it was green. This is where Long Hot Mike had been laid on the fence. Already dead, she was sure. Now that she knew the exact spot, she could see some dark stains in the dirt below the wires, browner than the soil, which was rather reddish. That had to be his blood. He had bled from a wound here. There wasn't much staining, though. So he probably wasn't killed here.

Where would that have been? If only she could get some evidence! Lulu had told her she had a cop nephew in Ant Bite. Could she work on him? She would need his name for that.

About two minutes after she came in the back door, her family burst through the front door. That is, Drew burst in. Ralph and Hortense followed more sedately.

"Did you have fun at the park?" Immy asked Drew.

Drew made her eyes big with enthusiasm and nodded vigorously. "There are swings and a slide and a merry-go-round and a jungle gym! All the stuff!"

It sounded pretty standard to Immy, but it made Drew happy. She beamed at her happy daughter.

"Anybody hungry?" Ralph asked.

"Oh, Lulu and Victor went out. It's like a date night for them, so we're on our own."

Ralph looked at Hortense and Immy knew he was waiting for her to volunteer to cook. Sometimes Immy wondered which he loved more, her mother's cooking, or her.

Hortense had plopped onto the couch. "Oh my, it was a lot of exercise at the park. I just want to sit for a bit."

"Why don't we go out, then? You won't have to cook, Mother. There aren't very many restaurants here, but they're pretty good and very cheap. Or, we could go to a neighboring town, say Ant Bite."

"Ant Bite?" shrieked Drew. "There's a town named Ant Bite? Do they have ants that bite you?"

"I'm sure they don't anymore. I think they must have had some once and named the town a long time ago."

"I wanna go there. I wanna see the ants. If there's any left."

"Where is it?" Ralph crossed the room to give Immy a hug.

"Not far." She whipped out her phone to see if she was telling the truth. She was relieved to see it was only about twenty miles away.

Ralph shrugged. "Okay. I'm hungry now. Anybody else?"

Hortense heaved herself off the couch to signify that she was ready.

"Wait. Baffroom." Drew ran toward that room and Ralph said he needed something from his car.

Immy took that opportunity to ask her mother about seeing her cousin. "How was Ouida, Mother?"

"She was quite strange. Very different from the first time I was there. I came to the door with the comestibles and she seemed reluctant to let me in. She took the package and went to the kitchen, and I assumed that was an invitation and followed her. However, she deposited my gift on her kitchen counter without a thank you, turned and went down the hall."

"Was she not raised very well?"

"She was raised in a perfectly fine manner. Being with these uncouth heathens in this town has obviously affected her. To complete my recitation, I followed her down the hall, but she entered a bedroom and closed the door."

"Wow! That was really rude."

"Quite. I left forthwith. I must, however, persist in inquiries in order to find out what has precipitated this change."

Immy was picturing her mother's delectable food sitting out on a counter.

Drew came running out of the bathroom and they all went outside. Ralph was talking on his cop radio thing, but cut the call as soon as they showed up.

"Guess what I just learned?" he said. "They caught the library thief."

"How did they do that?" Immy asked.

"His sister told on him. The robber was a little kid. He hid in the bookshelves while they closed up, then came out and took the money. He bragged about it to her and she did her civic duty."

"Oh my." Hortense gaped for a brief moment. "What will his punishment be?"

"Nothin' much. His daddy found the money and gave it back. He's banned from the library for a month."

"Big crime in Saltlick," Immy said. "Maybe that will make him want to read more? Being deprived for a month?"

Ralph looked doubtful. So did Hortense.

They all climbed into the van and Ralph drove. His truck would have had trouble holding all of them.

After half an hour he pulled into an unimpressive restaurant parking lot, with a sturdy metal railing, no doubt put there to prevent drunk cowboys from driving into the red-painted cement block front wall.

Drew grabbed her grandmother's hand and pulled her toward the door. Ralph caught Immy's shoulder and stopped her for a private question.

"Okay, why did you really want to go here? Is there someone here you need to see?"

Immy tried to blink innocently. "Not really." After all, she didn't even know the name of the guy. She did, however, hope to learn it tonight. He was on to her, though, and now she knew. She would have to be pretty darn stealthy.

The menu told of burgers, nachos, a Caesar salad, and beef barbecue. There was also a fairly full bar, by the looks of it.

She had the nachos, Drew wanted a burger, and Hortense and Ralph both had barbecue.

Halfway through the meal, she asked Ralph if he'd like another beer. "I'll get it," she volunteered, when he nodded, and she hopped up.

At the bar, she leaned in close to the woman who was serving and asked if she knew Lulu Henry's nephew, the police officer. She thought these two tiny towns were close enough together for everyone to know everyone else.

"Sure. That's him over there." She pointed with the frothing beer glass she had just filled from the tap.

Immy glanced in that direction and saw a small man wearing a denim shirt with his blue jeans, and a red cowboy hat. Out of uniform, obviously. Good. Ralph wouldn't know he was a cop when Immy talked to him. If she could manage that. She saw that his beer glass was almost full, so she would have to wait for him to return to the bar. "What's his name? I forget. Lulu told me to say hi to him."

"He's Hank. Hank Beasley. Some people call him Officer Beasley, like, if he's arresting them, but we usually call him Hank in here."

"Okay, thanks." She'd gotten a whole dissertation. She could use it for ammunition in her interrogation.

She carried Ralph's beer back and sipped hers until she saw Hank approaching the bar with an empty. After glugging the rest of hers, two thirds of the large glass, she jumped up and headed for the bar.

The server was just finishing drawing Hank's brew and was letting the foam calm down. Immy stood next to him, trying not to burp from all the beer she had just chugged.

"Hey, you're Lulu Henry's nephew, right?"

The server looked at her funny, since she knew that Immy knew who he was. Unless Immy had short-term memory loss. Immy ignored that.

He turned toward Immy and gave her a tentative smile, showing her a gold incisor. "Yep, that's me. What do you need?"

"I just want to say hi."

"Well, howdy. Tell Lulu hey and I'll be over there one of these days. It's been too long."

"Slap Out has had some trouble."

"I heard about that. A couple of murders."

"Yes. I've been hired by one of the suspects. Sorry, I should introduce myself. I'm Imogene Duckworthy, Private Eye."

He drew his head back an inch, impressed, she hoped.

"I'm having trouble getting any information from the Slap Out police force. Do you know which way they're leaning? What evidence they have against anybody?"

Too much. He drew all of his body farther back. "Sorry, I don't mess in their business unless they ask me to. Nope, don't know anything about it."

"Both bodies were found right behind Lulu and Victor's house.

We're staying there. With them. We're house guests there. Came in for the wedding because the groom's family is kin. It's pretty upsetting for all of us."

"I bet." He grabbed his mug and left for his table and the two companions there with him.

That had been a complete bust. Immy would kick herself in the rear if that were physically possible. She had come on way too strong. Oh well. She got her mug filled, visited the little girls', and returned to their table.

As soon as she sat down, Ralph asked her, "What was that?"

"What? What was what?" She batted her eyes. It didn't work.

"You bothering that guy. He didn't look happy about it."

"Oh, I thought he was somebody else. Someone I met in Slap Out. Everybody ready to go?"

They were, but she had a brand-new mug of beer, which Ralph pointed out.

"I decided I don't want it." Ralph was obviously overly suspicious, knew she wasn't telling him something, but he should be used to that, she thought.

Immy stood and walked to the door and they all followed. She didn't look to make sure, but they were there when she turned around at the van, so they had.

Twenty-Six

ALL THE WAY BACK TO SLAP OUT, IMMY ran through different scenarios in her mind. Different ways she could get some information on her Case. Nothing was viable. They were mostly just ideas for breaking and entering. Getting arrested and looking at the evidence room seemed to be the best one. If there was one. It was a small station. Maybe there was an evidence closet. Or evidence drawer. Those would make it easier. But she really didn't want to get arrested.

Ralph was driving carefully, since he'd had a couple of beers. Maybe Hortense should have driven. She had only had sweet tea. Immy was in the back, since Hortense just about had to sit up front. Immy kind of wanted to talk to Ralph, but it was hard from the back seat. Drew was chattering on and on about the subject of goats. She really wanted one. Immy wondered how it would work to have a pet pig and a pet goat. That was hard to picture. The little goat jumping on top of Marshmallow? Marshmallow lying down and crushing the goat? The goat butting Marshmallow, and everyone else? All the noise and commotion? And the slight stench. Which wasn't always slight.

She had a sudden thought. Long was dead. What would happen to his goats? She would have to ask Lulu or Victor. Maybe they could get one cheap. Or free. The fact that they ate poison ivy and kudzu meant a goat could earn its keep. She could rent it out, like Long told them about. They could get a larger one, not like Babalu. Surely

Marshmallow wouldn't roll over on it.

Drew was worn out, probably from the park, and she went to bed soon after they got to the house, as did Hortense, who was equally worn out.

So Ralph and Immy sat in the backyard, on the porch steps, each with one last beer, watching the gamboling goat and the frisky dogs that they had let out. The silly goat had leapt up and was hopping up and down on top of the little shelter. Immy wondered if she would break it. Or he. She couldn't remember what kind of goat this was. Babalu could denote either sex.

"I learned something, Ralph. You can't get electrocuted on an electric fence."

"Of course not. You can't die, but you can get a shock. It's better not to touch them. You thought it would kill you?"

"Well, they found Long Mike's body hanging on it. So I thought it killed him."

"Strange place to put a body."

"It is, isn't it? He was dead first, I guess."

"Was he tied to the fence? Fastened to it? I guess you could die of thirst or hunger if you were left that way for a few days."

"I don't think so. He couldn't have been there long."

"Why not?"

"Because we had…I saw him earlier in the day." She didn't feel like telling Ralph she'd had lunch with one of the most handsome men she'd ever seen. "I'm trying to figure out who would kill both of those guys."

"Didn't you say they were rowdy? Beat people up in bars? Had gone around doing a lot of damage?"

"Well, yes. The three of them."

"Who's the third one?"

"Wyatt. Wyatt Harbor." With a sharp intake of breath, she realized that Wyatt would probably be next. "We should see if he's okay."

"Why?"

"Because he might get murdered too."

"Unless he killed the other two."

The wind picked up a bit and shifted and brought them a whiff of sulfur from the wells. She needed to hire an operative to tail Wyatt. That would serve a dual function. It might save his life, or it might reveal him as the killer. "I don't think my client would even want to kill them. But I have to prove he didn't."

Ralph shook his head. He didn't think much of her "case," she knew.

"You don't have to be that way. It's my first case. You could be supportive." For sure, she wouldn't hire Ralph. If only Drew were older. Immy closed her eyes and imagined her daughter as a teen, or maybe a young woman, going into business with her. Doing some filing, typing up reports, and taking care of surveillance when she couldn't do it. She would teach Drew all about disguises.

"I'm sorry, Immy, but I don't see any way for you to work on your *case*. You don't know these people and you don't know your client."

Darn it! He was absolutely right. She knew something of Junior's and Long's backgrounds, but she needed more. She would call Loryetta in the morning. The energetic goat drummed its hooves on the roof of his shelter again, then jumped down, nearly landing on a dog. She thought it was Lucy, the little Corgi.

"Anyway, we're leaving tomorrow."

That made her sit up straight. "Who is *we*?"

"Us. I have to get back. I have a job."

"I know about those. I have one too. Take your truck back. Take Mom and Drew, too, if you want, but I'm staying here with the van." She got up and went inside, slamming the door a bit to make her point.

After she got into bed, pretty thoroughly bitten by mosquitoes, she lay awake, waiting for Ralph to come lie beside her, and hoping he would decide they couldn't fit in his truck, so he should stay longer. And help her.

When he kept not coming into the room, she decided she would do one last bit of snooping. She pulled her clothes back on and left through the back door and out the side gate without encountering anyone, especially Ralph.

When she got to the Newberry house, she rang the bell and waited.

After a bit, Ouida came to the door. "Who are you? We don't need any."

"I'm Imogene, Hortense's daughter. Your cousin."

"Oh yes, she was here earlier."

It seemed like the woman was in a daze. "Do you mind if I come in? Mother was worried about you."

"She needn't be." But Ouida led the way into the house.

They ended up in the kitchen. Immy saw Hortense's offerings, still on the counter. Maybe they'd still be okay. "Cousin Ouida, do you mind if I put my mother's food in your fridge?"

Ouida gave her a blank stare. Maybe she didn't even see the food. Immy had to remember that she had just lost her son. Immy stuck the food into the refrigerator, shifting some things and setting the new stuff on top of the many other bereavement food items, mostly casseroles, already there.

"Can I get you a glass of water? Some coffee?"

Ouida looked at Immy as if she had just woken up. "Maybe coffee."

The woman went into the living room and sat on the couch while Immy explored the kitchen, looking for the makings. She found an old-fashioned percolator, some ground coffee, and some filters. While it brewed, she went to sit with the poor woman. At least she hadn't gone to the bedroom and shut the door.

"Are you alone here?" It was very quiet. She couldn't hear any other sounds in the house.

"I am."

"Where is Mr. Newberry?" Out killing Wyatt?

"He left. He went to his brother's place."

"I'm sorry. Do you need someone to stay with you?"

"No, I'm fine. It's better that he's gone right now. Neither of us are good company."

It was a good thing to say, but she didn't understand how a man could leave his wife when their son had just been murdered.

"I understand. And let me tell you how sorry I am for the terrible loss. Such a shock."

Ouida focused her eyes on Immy's face for the first time. "You can't possibly know. No one can."

She thought maybe Long's relatives might, but he didn't seem to have any.

"Is there anything I can do for you?"

"You're making coffee. I appreciate that."

"Oh good. Let me check on it."

When Immy came back to the room with a cup and saucer, Ouida immediately started sipping, blowing on the liquid to cool it. Was she taking care of herself?

"Please remember to eat and drink. You don't want to get sick. On top of everything else."

"No, I suppose not."

"Have the police told you anything? Are they finding out who did this awful thing?" She felt a little bit bad, pumping the suffering mother, but she couldn't pass up this chance.

"They say they have some leads."

Immy sat up straight. "They do? That's good. Did they tell you what they were?"

"Well, Eccles."

"Oh, yes, Eccles." That wasn't a bit helpful. "Any other leads?"

Ouida shook her head. Her hands started to shake and she set the coffee cup down, spilling some into the saucer. The woman was in bad shape.

"I'm sorry. I should go. Please call me if you need anything. I'm going to be in town for a few days." Again, Immy acutely felt the absence of business cards. She wrote her name and number on a page from her notebook, tore it out, and set it on the table, next to the cup, avoiding the wet place where some coffee had sloshed out.

When she returned to the Henrys' house, Ralph was in bed. She crept in next to him, wondering what she'd tell him in the morning when he asked where she had been.

When Immy woke up, Ralph had already left the bed. His side was cold. She stumbled out of the bedroom, tying her bathrobe and looking for him. Surely he hadn't left. His truck door slammed. She could hear it because the front door was open.

Hortense was making scrambled eggs with onions and peppers, and some sausage, it smelled like, and Drew sat at the table expectantly.

Immy hadn't realized that Lulu and Victor were going to spend the night out, but there had been no sign of them last night and she didn't see them this morning. She went down the hallway. Their bedroom door was open, so she could peek in through the open door. Nope, they weren't here. Since they were slight suspects in her mind, she hoped they weren't doing anything nefarious.

She went to the front door just as Ralph was returning.

"All packed," he said.

"What do you mean? Who's all packed?"

"We are. Everyone but you."

"You're really all going to squeeze into your truck for hours?"

"It's not that long a drive."

He pushed past her, went to the kitchen, and started dishing himself some eggs. Hortense was just buttering the toast as he and Immy entered the room.

"Oh good, you're both here. Sit and eat." Hortense held out a plate for Immy.

Immy narrowed her eyes at the scene. Yes, she was hungry and everything smelled delicious, but she didn't feel like being with these people who were abandoning her. "So you're all just going to leave?"

"We came for a nuptial ceremony, dear, and that never transpired. There is no longer any reason to remain here. In fact, we have grossly overstayed. If there were something more I could do for my cousin, I would gladly delay the departure to accomplish it, but that doesn't seem to be the case."

"Mother, I think you're right, but she can call on me if she needs help. I left her my number. I'm well aware that her child has been murdered. Are you aware that I've been charged with solving the Case?"

Ralph raised his head. "No, you haven't. You've been hired to look for evidence to clear one suspect."

Rats! He was right. Immy huffed at him, holding her plate, deciding where to sit. "Well, the best way to do that is to find out who did it. Duh."

Ralph shook his head, then lowered it toward his plate again. Immy carried her breakfast to the backyard. Hortense came to the door to speak to her.

"Dear, do you have any knowledge of the whereabouts of our host and hostess? I'm beginning to worry about them."

"It's still early. Maybe they're sleeping in at a motel. One located in a town other than Slap Out, it is to be hoped. I think we'd hear if something happened to them."

But, would they? If Lulu and Victor had been in a car wreck, were in the hospital, or dead, would anyone think to notify their houseguests? Maybe not. How would she find out?

She didn't have to wonder for very long. They had all eaten inside after Immy returned to the table, and Hortense had cleaned up the dishes. Immy brought hers to the counter to add to the dishwasher just as the Henrys walked in the front door.

"Oh, there you are!" Hortense almost ran over to hug them. "We were so worried about you."

"You were?" Lulu took a step back. "I told you we were spending a night to ourselves."

"Yes, you did," Immy assured her. "We just weren't clear on what that meant, I guess. Like the evening, or overnight. Anyway, I hope you had a wonderful time."

"We did! We went clear into Mammoth and stayed at a motel."

Immy and Hortense gave each other looks of relief.

"Had dinner and a movie. It was a wonderful break." Lulu smiled the whole time she was telling them this.

Immy didn't see any luggage. In fact, Lulu was wearing the same clothes she had had on the day before. Maybe they just took toothbrushes and undies. She hoped they had taken toothbrushes and undies. She certainly wasn't going to ask about that.

"We're about to take off," Ralph said, stepping over to Victor and shaking his hand. "Thanks for the hospitality. Mighty kind of you."

"Have a safe trip back," Lulu said as she made her way to the kitchen to feed the dogs. That had been the last thing she had done before they left, too. Victor went out to tend to the goat.

"Oh, do you know who's taking care of the goats?" Immy asked.

"We only have one and we take care of him," Lulu said, a puzzled expression on her face.

"No, I mean Tuttle's goats. I hope someone is taking care of them."

Lulu tilted her head. "I wonder. Maybe we should check on that. You go along. I'll do that."

"Uh, I'm not leaving with them. I have to finish my job." She looked for a bit of dismay on Lulu's face, but didn't see any. She would offer anyway. "If I need to stay somewhere else, that's no problem. Just tell me."

"No, but it is a problem. The other place is that horrible Motel Four."

That was true. She could stay there, but wouldn't like it.

"Don't even think about it. Stay here as long as you need to. You won't bother us at all."

Immy couldn't tell from Victor's non-expression if he was in favor of her staying or not. "Oh, thank you so much." That was a relief, having a place to stay. Along with Lulu and Victor not being injured or dead. In spite of her folks abandoning her, the day was looking up. Maybe she could find the real killer soon and join them in Saltlick.

She went outside to tell her family goodbye. They were all squeezed inside the truck. Hortense and Drew waved and blew kisses. Ralph didn't. Immy tried not to fume. If he wasn't going to accept her for who she was, a PI, she would have to rethink their relationship. For now, she had to shove that aside. If she didn't, she would have to find another place to live and she wasn't going to face that right now. Not ever, she hoped.

The truck vanished around a distant corner and she went to her room to figure out what her next move should be.

Twenty-Seven

AFTER PONDERING AND DOODLING FOR HALF AN HOUR in her room, then wandering outside a bit, Immy was getting desperate. She had nothing. Not clues, no confessions, nothing. She had to get something. The scheme she had dreamed up was not practical. It was scary and dangerous. But it was all she had. It would be better to implement it at night, but it was morning now and she couldn't wait.

"I'm going out," she called to Lulu as she left by the front door. "Don't wait up if I'm late."

She left before she could read Lulu's expression. It might be one of alarm, and Immy didn't want to see that.

Leaving the van a few blocks away, she walked to the street the jail was on and strolled past it twice. Once going one way, then again after turning and going the other way. No one was visible on the street or sidewalk either time. She couldn't see any cameras, but she didn't really know what they looked like.

Was anyone even inside the building? She would have to go around to the back to see if any cars were there. Peeking around the corner at the parking lot, she saw two of them. That would have to do. She would have to assume that someone was inside.

Before she had set out, she had prepared, so her purse held a large, heavy rock from the oil field. That darn police station was almost all wall. The only window in the front was the glass door and a couple of little slitty glass panels on either side of it that probably wouldn't even break. The door, however, was the middle glass piece, and it was fairly large, as targets go. She hoped the glass wasn't unbreakable, or bulletproof, or something annoying like that.

For her plan to work, she had to be caught. Someone had to see her breaking the glass. For some reason, no one was out right then. Eventually, though, a young couple came out of the real estate office across the street.

That was her signal. It was time. She took the rock, cocked her arm back, and threw the rock through the glass with a loud grunt, as loud as she could make it.

"Look at that, Jerrell! She just threw that rock through there!"

Jerrell came running at Immy. She made a lame attempt to escape, for appearances, to continue her plan, and he caught up to her easily. "Hey, where do you think you're going?"

Immy didn't think he had to grab her that roughly. After he took hold of her arm, he squeezed it, hard. And shook it, a lot. Then hauled her back and through the broken door, stepping on the glass shards that were littering the sidewalk and crunching them under their shoes.

By this time, two officers had just about reached them from inside.

"Hey!" One of them echoed Jerrell. "What do you think you're doing?"

"She just threw a rock and broke y'all's door."

"I'll take over," said the uniform nearest Immy. Unfortunately he was Officer Powell, the one who had questioned her at the oil field. He took her arm and was much more gentle than Jerrell had been, she was glad to note. He led her through the station to a chair beside his own desk.

Now she would have to play this just right. She had to be guilty enough to have to spend some time here, but not enough to get charged with anything. Maybe she hadn't thought this through well enough. She hadn't prepared a script. How exactly would she do this part?

"What in the world do you think you were doing?" He sounded

pretty stern. And upset. "You know you'll have to pay for that damage."

Oh. She hadn't thought of that. And Ralph and Hortense were both gone. She didn't have much money on her, and Hortense had the credit cards. It was probably something she could mail in from home later. Maybe.

Inspiration struck. Maybe this would work. She straightened as tall as she could in the chair. "You are holding evidence that pertains to my client and I want it released to him."

"Your client? You're a lawyer?"

"I am a private detective."

"Huh." He didn't look convinced. "Who do you think your client is?"

That made her mad. Since she wasn't handcuffed, happily, she opened her purse and put her hand inside. "I don't *think* anything."

"Hold it!" Officer Powell put his hand on his weapon, in the holster on his belt.

"I'm showing you proof of what I'm saying."

He grabbed her purse and, she assumed, looked for a gun. Not finding one, he handed it back to her. "Okay, what are you showing me?"

She pulled out her certificate. It was too bad she had had to fold it to fit in her purse. Maybe she could get another copy to frame, later. It wouldn't look good hanging on a wall with a nice frame and being all creased.

When she thrust it at him, he said, "Okay, you have a PI certificate. What about your client?"

The contract wasn't in her purse. Maybe it should be. "I don't have the contract with me, but that information is confidential."

"So how am I going to know what evidence you're talking about?"

That was actually a good question. This was hopeless.

"This is my first Case. I've just become a private eye. I'm having trouble getting any information at all. Could you tell me what your clues are? What your evidence is? And who you suspect right now?"

"No, not really. Are you sure you can't tell me who you're trying to clear? I could let you know whether that person is a serious suspect of not."

She wondered if he should even do that. Maybe he just wanted very badly to get rid of her.

"I'm going to pay for the damage. I should get something for that."

"That's not how this works at all." He shook his head and stared at her for a moment. "Your first case, huh? I suppose you hope to have another one someday."

"Oh yes, I do. I really do." Was he weakening? She must not seem too eager.

"At the moment, we have a number of suspects, but no clear front-runner. Whoever your client is, he or she is probably not off the hook." He was a nice man, as far as cops go, she thought. She knew lots of nice ones and just a few who weren't.

"But what's your evidence?"

"Are you listening to me? I can't tell you that." He paused for a moment. "Why did you break that glass? Were you going to sneak in here and look around?"

"No, that's not what I was going to do. Not exactly. I was going to get caught and then be held for a while so I could look around when no one was noticing." She might as well tell him. It wasn't going to work, anyway.

After he got her address, so he could send her the bill, he stood, shook his head again, and escorted her out the front door, kicking aside the glass shards and trying to avoid stepping on them.

Plodding toward the van that was still where she had left it, a couple of blocks away, she tried to formulate a new plan. She was completely stuck. She opened the door and climbed in, then sat for a few minutes, trying to make her brain start working. She couldn't even think of any lists to make. But Eccles Justice had already paid her a fee, so she had to do something constructive. She had to earn it. There was no way around that.

She remembered that time when she and her mother had started a fire at the Saltlick police station. That would have been a better idea than breaking the door.

The only thing to do now, was to start over. She would think this thing through from the beginning. She probably knew everything she was going to know, and she would just have to figure out what had happened. She would think everything through, starting at the beginning.

The wedding. No, the day before the wedding. No, before that. The three hellions, Ned Junior, Long and Wyatt had had a barroom brawl and deeply, fatally, injured someone. If Junior were still alive, he would now have been charged with the death of Claude Barrelson. But Claude had died after Junior was dead, so it was unlikely his parents were taking revenge before their son expired. They were probably glued to his hospital bed.

The next thing she knew about was the rehearsal dinner. All three of the men were there, as were two of their fathers. Long Hot Mike Tuttle's relatives weren't there. They either didn't run in the same circle as the two rich men, or lived in another town, or were all dead, as Long had implied, although she knew she couldn't believe what he told her. The other father, Sydney Harbor, wasn't in the same league as the bride and groom's fathers either, money-in-the-bank-wise.

Loryetta was on the verge of calling the ceremony off. The three younger guys went out carousing after the rehearsal dinner.

But wait, something else happened. The father of the groom, Ned Newberry, announced that he was much wealthier now, because of the oil rights he had cheated Wyatt's dad out of.

How could Wyatt Harbor go out with Ned Junior after that? But he did. Maybe he didn't care about how humiliated and angry his father was. Immy remembered driving past the place where they were and seeing Wyatt's father sitting near a window. Seething? Planning to kill the groom? Wouldn't he more likely want to kill the groom's father? Or would he think it better to inflict the pain of losing a son on him? Maybe he thought he'd lost his own son to the hell-raising trio.

A smattering of rain started hitting her windshield, as clouds cut off the sun, like closing the curtains in a bedroom. Immy had been sitting slumped over the steering wheel, but she raised her head with a sudden thought. Someone had mentioned that the two, Junior and his father, would look the same in the dark. Wouldn't it be more likely that Junior's dad would be in the oil field? Checking out his possessions? The sources of his wealth? Maybe even the morning of the wedding?

Was this something that could tell her something? That he had been the intended target?

There was one big problem. What on earth would Junior be doing there? He seemed like a playboy, living off his father's wealth, but not concerned about the origins of it. Or was Immy just making up what he was like, because she had only met him for a very short time? Maybe he was also a businessman who kept track of the family holdings.

She continued the timeline. The next morning, before anyone knew Junior was dead, Loryetta was having sex with Wyatt in the church. Was this his way of sticking it to the Justice family for what they had done to his? To him and his father? That was quite possible. It also meant that sticking it to Junior by killing him would be difficult to manage, time-wise.

Immy had found out that Eccles had gotten to the church early, so he probably didn't kill his partner's son. And he would have no reason to, none that Immy could figure out.

Okay, she fished her notebook out of her purse and started writing, making a list of everyone who might want to kill Ned Junior.

In a column at the left she put:

Wyatt Harbor

Sydney Harbor

The Barrelsons

Loryetta?

Ouida? The man's own mother?

In a column at the right, she put everyone who could have done it:

Wyatt Harbor

Sydney Harbor

The Barrelsons?

This made it seem simple. But now it got more complicated because Long was dead, too. That had to tie in somehow.

If the same person killed them both, why? If Long killed Junior, why? If one of the Harbors killed Junior, father or son, why would they kill Long?

There had to be an answer somewhere. The police didn't seem to have it yet. But neither did she.

Still pretty discouraged, with nowhere else to go, Immy went back to the Henrys'.

Lulu sat at the kitchen table opening the mail. She slit open a few envelopes that looked like bills, then picked up a thick square envelope. Immy thought it looked like a wedding invitation. She didn't want to go to another one of those for a long time.

After Lulu removed the card inside, her face crumpled and a tear squeezed from her blinking eyes.

"What is it?" Immy asked.

"Funerals. Plural. I hate funerals. They're going to hold a double ceremony for Junior and Long."

"Oh. That seems strange."

"Well, Long doesn't have any family here anymore. So I guess that's nice that the Newberrys are doing that for him."

Maybe Long hadn't lied to her at all. He really didn't have family. Not here, anyway. If he had any anywhere, they weren't able to arrange his service.

Twenty-Eight

Would the dual funeral give Immy a chance to observe the perps, to find the killer? Or killers?

"When is the funeral?" she asked.

Lulu threw the notice onto the kitchen table and sat back in her chair. "It's tomorrow. This is awfully fast. I'm surprised I got this in the mail in time to go to it."

Could she make excuses to stick around until then? Should she? It was beginning to feel like she was abusing the hospitality of her hosts.

Lulu heaved herself up with a sigh. "All of this business makes me so tired. But I do have to feed Babalu, and clean the yard, no matter how tired I feel."

"You really do keep it nice, picking up all the dog poop. Drew never once got into any."

That made Lulu smile and also made her look less weary. "That's good. I would hate for that to happen." She headed for the plastic bucket of goat food supplements they were keeping on the counter for now, and picked that up. There was a large bag of hay in the pantry and she headed there first.

"Can I help you?" Immy wanted to offset her extended stay by being a little useful. She could do that, at least. After Lulu grabbed an armful of hay, Immy took the bucket from her and followed her outside.

Lulu strewed the hay around on the ground as Babalu came running.

Before he got too far, she reached into the bucket Immy held and sprinkled a scoop of the supplement pellets on top. The ravenous goat chowed down on everything.

Again, Immy got a whiff of the sulfur from the nearby oil field. "I guess you get used to that smell?"

"Not really. It used to be so nice here, in our private yard. We always wish those wells weren't there. Ever since they started drilling on that land. The pumps are noisy, besides the smell. Just a nuisance."

The setting sun caught on the back fence and threw a gleam in Immy's eye. For the first time, she noticed how shiny that portion of the fencing was. The sides were duller, more weathered.

"Is that part of the fence new?" she asked.

"Well, yes. The rest of the fence has been here a long time, but when they started drilling out there, we had to put some new fencing across that part of the property."

"Is that your land?" Lulu made it sound like someone was drilling on her land.

"We don't think of it that way anymore."

Immy wanted more information about that back land, but Lulu's cell phone rang. "It's Victor," she said and went to the far part of the yard to talk to him.

Had everyone in Slap Out bought land? And had they all been swindled out of the mineral rights? She wondered how they had all been talked into it by Newberry and Justice. How many people's land were they drilling on, anyway? Those two seemed to be slick operators. She thought it was a wonder that both of them hadn't been knocked off before this.

Immy went into the house, leaving Lulu outside talking to her husband, set the bucket back in the corner of the kitchen counter, and headed toward the bedroom. She glanced at the notice of the funeral ceremony first and saw that the ceremony was at one o'clock at the church. At the same place the wedding was supposed to have been.

If everyone in town had been swindled in land deals, then everyone in town was a suspect for the murders. IF the murders had anything to do with the land deals. The more Immy thought about it, the more she was convinced that Ned Newberry was the intended victim. He was the one who had made the horrible, tasteless announcement the night before the wedding. That would surely make him a target. It even made sense that he would be out inspecting his wells before the service. The father of the groom wasn't as important in a wedding as a lot of others were. He didn't have to be there early, or have any duties. She hadn't asked anyone when he got to the church.

Okay, that explained the death of the first victim. Mistaken identity and revenge on the family for being cheated. Even if it probably should have been the father, not the son. But the second murder? Long Tuttle? Was he in the wrong place at the wrong time?

She cast back on the conversation she had had with him. He'd been upset at being questioned for hours. What was that he had said? Because he left the bachelor party early? Where did he go? She wished she had asked him. She couldn't now.

She was close to figuring out the whys, but nowhere near knowing who the whos were.

Passing the kitchen table on the way to the guest room, she read the notice one more time. Could she attend? She thought she would like to. Well, she wouldn't actively like it, funerals were not fun, but it might be a place to gather information. Maybe someone, in grief, would let their guard down, and clues would tumble out. And she could be there to catch them. And maybe she was dreaming right now.

Immy had retreated to the guest room, but she heard the front door slam and assumed Victor had come home. She opened her door and started to come out, but Lulu's raised voice made her hesitate.

"What do you think you're doing, Victor Henry?"

"Lulu. Just leave me be. I needed to let off some steam."

"You're no worse than those thieves, drinking like that."

"Ha! If I was like them, we'd be better than them. We'd be rich."

Immy could see them through the crack of her door, just barely ajar, which gave her a view of part of the living room, around the corner. Victor stumbled through the room on his way to the kitchen. Lulu stopped and quietly seethed for a moment, then followed him. She waited a few long moments. Maybe it was safe to come out now, and pretend she hadn't heard the argument.

But just as she entered the kitchen, where Victor had dropped into a chair, there was an eruption.

"What in the hell is this?" He was waving the funeral notice card.

"It's what it looks like, Vic."

Immy backed through the doorway a bit.

"Why the fuck do they think we would want to go to this? It's bad enough I was forced to go to his wedding. Now I have to go to his goddamn funeral, too?"

"No, you don't have to. But it would look funny if you didn't."

Victor, having caught sight of her, swung his head around and faced her. "Immy, you're still here."

"Yes. I can leave soon."

"Hmm."

At first she had thought he was upset to see her, but he'd dropped that.

"Is there anything to eat?" This last was directed at his wife.

Lulu silently poured some canned soup into a pan and started the stove. The air in the kitchen lay heavy with tension bearing down on all three of them.

Victor didn't say anything else, but Immy got a bad feeling coming from him, bad vibrations. He was full of anger, that was obvious. It was understandable, but she didn't want to get in the way of that. It could be dangerous for her.

The silence grew heavier. Immy had to say something. "You know what? I can pack up and go now. I think I've probably stayed too long. You've been *so* nice. We all enjoyed the hospitality."

They didn't seem to have enough energy for her. There was no reply. She quickly threw her stuff together, walked through the silent house, and got into the van.

Where on earth would she go? She had no idea. No way was she leaving town, though.

Twenty-Nine

SHE WOULD HAVE TO BUNK AT THAT HORRIBLE, rundown, dirty, buggy motel. There was no place else she could go. Staying out of town wouldn't work. She needed to be here, in the middle of the action. Besides, all the other motels would cost more than Motel Four did, and her budget was tight, having received only the deposit so far. She would have to think about raising that for her next Case.

At least there was someone at the counter in the office this time, so checking in was quick and easy. And still cheap. That was a virtue to offset everything else.

The van always held a few stray plastic grocery bags and she decided to bring in only the bare necessities in one of them. It was better to expose only what was necessary to the bedbugs and the cockroaches that were almost certainly there, hiding. She crawled into the back of the van and opened her suitcase to select these few things. Toiletries and a nightgown. And some clean underwear for the next day. She would also need something fairly nice looking, and subdued, to wear to the double funeral. She had brought along wedding clothes and jeans and t-shirts. It would have to be the outfit she wore to the rehearsal dinner, her new jeans, a blue sweater, and nice blue boots. Those clothes hadn't been worn for more than a few hours. Blue was not black, but it should be an okay funeral color, she thought.

An unwelcome sound on the roof of the van meant it had just started raining. Why couldn't it have waited another five minutes? She tried to wait out the shower in the van, but it wasn't a shower. It was a deluge. Finally, she put another plastic bag over her head, held the one with her things in it tightly closed, and dashed into her room.

There were clean towels and, she was glad to find out, they were thick enough to dry her off. Just barely.

Once she was settled with her stuff in the room, she tried calling Ralph. He didn't pick up. Neither did her mother. Were they both mad at her? Still? They should have cooled off on the ride back home.

She was chilled from the rain, and still a little damp, so she strolled into the bathroom. The tub didn't look bad. She swiped her hand along the sides and nothing came off, so it was clean enough. A long soak would feel good and would warm her up. The option of going out drinking, like Victor, to let off steam, wasn't really a good one for her when she was feeling down. And when it was pouring outside. Although the thought did enter her mind. Anyway, she just wasn't the type. But a good long bath would help.

When she had been in the tub for probably a half hour or so, her phone rang. She had left it on the floor next to the tub so it was easy to reach over the edge and pick it up. It was Ralph, she was happy to see!

"Hey! How was the drive home?"

"We're going tomorrow. We decided to stay in Fort Worth tonight."

"Why? The drive isn't that long?"

"I told Drew I'd take her to Six Flags, so we've been there for a few hours."

No wonder they hadn't answered their phones. They went to Six Flags without her? How could they? "Oh, that's nice. I hope you had fun." She cut off the call. She would need more hot water and a longer soak. Too bad she didn't have an alcoholic drink handy.

Ralph didn't call again. Hortense didn't call at all. And she took her cue from them. They could just be that way. She had a mission. A job. A Case.

In the morning it was clear and sunny. She drove to Gordo's for pancakes. The town didn't look any better for having been through a cleansing, all-night rain, but it didn't look any worse. After she ate, she went back to her dingy room and got her good—well her better—clothes on.

She had slept on top of the spread where, she hoped, it was safer than on the sheets. There were no bedbug bites on her and she hadn't seen any. But she hadn't looked for them. Better to just not lift up the spread, she thought.

The service was in the same church as the wedding, so she knew how to get there. She showed up a little before one and the sanctuary was more than half full already. This event seemed to be a big community draw.

She was shepherded to the front to view the bodies. A quick glance was all she could manage before turning away to find a seat. She didn't like to look at dead bodies. And she hadn't even known these well when they were alive. Not for more than a few hours.

The Newberrys, Mr. and Mrs., were in the front. There didn't seem to be a separate seating area for family, like at a funeral home. One very old woman was with them. Probably a grandmother. Probably Ned's mother. Hortense would have known if Ouida's mother was alive, and she had said Ouida was all alone. She spotted Wyatt sitting by himself about halfway back. His father probably had not come. She scooted in next to him.

"Are you doing okay?" she asked. He had to be terribly conflicted about all of this.

He shrugged. "Better than my dad is."

She hoped Sydney Harbor wasn't in a bar right now. That would look so bad. If he really was the killer it would have been better to come to the funerals.

"Are you with the Henrys?" He looked around for them.

"No, I came by myself." She didn't want to explain that she had moved out of the house because of the bad atmosphere. And because she had been there too long. And because her family had left. It was something more than that, if she let herself think about it. Victor had seemed downright scary last night.

"They might not come," Wyatt said. "Victor about bust a gut when those wells came in, and he had just bought that land about a month before that."

"So he was pretty upset?"

"He sure was. I thought he was going to go after Ned Newberry a couple of times when they ran into each other in a few places around town."

"Oh, there they are." Immy watched Lulu march to the front for the required viewing, her face solidly set. It was either solemn or grim, Immy couldn't exactly tell which. That journey to the caskets didn't seem to be required for Victor. He took a seat in a pew in the back and didn't go to the front at all. It was pretty obvious, Immy thought, that he was pouting. Or fuming.

Wyatt leaned over and whispered, "I bet half the people here wanted to do what Victor did, just sit."

"Why is that?"

"You know why. Those two were not well liked. Hell, I'm not either. I kind of think I'm lucky I'm still alive."

That was true. She had even thought about that last statement. His two good buddies, his fellow hell-raisers, were both lying in the front of the church on soft silk cushions. Cold cushions.

The funeral was mercifully short. The minister probably knew that most of the congregation (did you call it that for a funeral, she wondered, or was it an audience?) didn't want to be there. The praise for Ned Junior and Long wasn't high, maybe medium high, maybe lukewarm. He dwelt, rather, on the fact that their lives had been taken too soon, cut too short. No one could argue with that. They should have both lived a lot longer. Even if no one wanted them to.

When the service was over, Immy felt she had to say something to Wyatt. He had shed a few silent tears. "I'm sorry for your loss. And I hope your dad is going to be okay."

She added, to herself, *unless he killed them*. Seeing how broken up Wyatt was, though, she wondered if Harbor would do that to his son, kill his friends. How was their relationship, she wondered. Much as she wanted to pump Wyatt, this wasn't the time or place.

She was able to scoot out ahead of the crowd. None of the Newberry family had even made it to the door for the condolence line yet.

After driving around the corner, she felt like she really wanted to talk to Ralph. Even if he had gone to Six Flags without her. She could probably make him take her, just the two of them, another time. The more she thought about that, the more she liked the idea. Ralph could shoot those targets, or toss those coins, and win her a big stuffed animal. Then she would walk around with it, but Drew would get it when they went home. Drew would love it and wouldn't be upset about not going with them. Right. So, talk to Ralph.

There was a problem, though. Her phone was dead. Out of juice. Much as she didn't want to return to Motel Four right then, not until she had to go there, she had to get her charger. Being without a phone was like being naked. She dashed in to get it, hoping to plug it into the van, but didn't find it. It wasn't in her suitcase, still in the back of the vehicle, either. She had to climb in there to rummage through the luggage.

Shoot! She must have left it plugged into the socket in the guest room at Lulu and Victor's. There wasn't anything she would less rather do right now than return to their house, but she would have to.

Thirty

How soon would the Henrys be home from the funeral, she wondered? They hadn't wanted to be there. Maybe they'd be home by now. Or maybe they'd gone out to eat. Tentatively, slowly, unwillingly, she drove across town to their place. Someone was there. Or were they? There was only one car in the driveway. Maybe they had both gone in the other one. That would make sense. So maybe they weren't home.

Immy crept to the front door, not knowing why she wanted to be so stealthy. It just seemed she should. A person should be careful when breaking and entering. She knew that. She turned the knob and pushed the front door. It was unlocked. Could she sneak in and get the charger? Then sneak out and not have to talk to anyone? Discussing the funeral was low on her to-do list right now. This would not be breaking, just entering, she was pretty sure.

She had to pass the kitchen, going down the hallway to get to the guest room. Lulu was at the table, but wasn't seeing anybody. Her head was down on the table, resting on her hands. Was she sleeping? Tired? In despair?

Victor must be out in the other car. It looked like Immy would be able to sneak in and sneak back out.

She was able to get into the guest room silently. There was her charger, in the socket. Bending over to unplug it, she knocked over the lamp on the dresser. It fell onto the dresser, not the floor, so maybe it hadn't made enough noise for Lulu to hear.

But when Immy straightened up and turned around, Lulu was in the doorway. It had made enough noise, that was obvious.

"I didn't hear you come in." There wasn't anything accusatory in Lulu's tone, but Immy thought there should have been. That was a relief. She had just entered their home without permission. Maybe Lulu forgot she moved out?

"I…I left my charger here." She held it up for Lulu to see. Then she set the lamp upright. "Sorry I knocked the lamp over." She was relieved that it hadn't broken. "I think it's okay.

"How long have you been here?"

"About two minutes. I just came in and I was going to leave and not bother you. I can leave now and not come back. Honest. I haven't left anything else here."

"No, that's okay. You just surprised me."

That was a pretty easy-going attitude, Immy thought. If she caught someone sneaking into her house, she would be plain mad.

"Would you like some coffee? A Coke?"

And she wouldn't offer them anything to drink, either. Or invite them to stick around. "I…I really should be going."

"Are you driving back home today?" Her face held no expression. She was unreadable.

Immy had time to get there before dark. Maybe she should.

Lulu didn't wait for an answer. "Would Drew like to have Babalu?"

"Uh, I'm sure she would. But Babalu belongs to you."

"I don't want anything that Long Tuttle used to own." Now it held expression, a lot of it. There was also dislike coming through in her words as well as her face. Her mouth was twisted and ugly when she said his name. She spit out the word "Tuttle."

"You don't like him? Didn't like him?"

Lulu shook her head. "I wish we hadn't taken that goat."

"Doesn't Victor like the goat? He built the little shelter and everything."

"Neither of us wants anything to remind us of him. Or the Newberrys."

Immy didn't see how the goat would remind anyone of the Newberrys. "I can't take your new pet. That wouldn't be right."

"It would be exactly right." Lulu sounded as firm about this as Immy had ever heard her.

The front door banged open and Immy heard someone reeling in with uneven steps. They both went to the kitchen as Victor entered it on the other side, from the living room, staggering drunk. Immy stayed to the rear of Lulu. He seemed kind of scary. His expression was an ugly scowl. It reminded Immy of Lulu's demeanor when she had talked about Long just now. And the Newberrys.

"What's she doing here? Come to spy on us? Dig up dirt?"

"Victor, she just came back to get her phone charger. And now she's just leaving. But, well, I wondered if we should give the goat to her. For her daughter. Then we would be rid of it."

He made his way to a kitchen chair and sat. "Yeah, that might be good. Get rid of it. Don't need any reminders around." These words were milder.

"Hush now." She patted his shoulder and turned to Immy. "Immy, let's see how we can do this."

Immy didn't see how they could. How would she transport a goat in her van? It would be all over the place, climbing on the seats, the headrests, probably the dashboard.

Lulu took her hand and pulled her toward the front door. "First of all, we need a carrier."

"Do you have one?"

They got into Lulu's car and started driving. This was bizarre. It was too quiet. Immy had to fill the silence.

"I guess Babalu isn't like a child."

Lulu gave her a quizzical look.

"I mean, the dogs are your children. Like your children. You treat them and love them like children."

"They are our children, you're right."

"But Babalu didn't make the cut. Did you ever think about having children?" Immy clamped her lips shut. Had she really said that? It was a horrible thing to say to people with no children. Maybe they had tried for years. Maybe Lulu had miscarried one or more.

"Oh yes." That was her complete answer. She didn't elaborate any more.

Immy shut up for the rest of the short, uncomfortable drive. She wanted to tell Lulu to turn around and take her to her van. Then she would leave and never come back. But Lulu was as scary now as Victor had just been.

They drove to Tractor Supply and, sure enough, there was a carrier that looked the right size. It would fit a very large dog, or a small goat. Maybe a medium goat, even. Immy offered, but Lulu paid for it and they wrestled it into her trunk, driving to the house with the trunk lid open. It fit just fine into the van, of course, through the big side doors.

In about five minutes, Lulu and Victor had put the goat into the cage and stashed the bag of hay and the bucket of supplements beside it. Victor worked efficiently, even as drunk as he was. When everything was loaded, he stepped back with a big smile, staggering only a little bit.

"There, we're rid of that." Why did they want to get rid of it so badly all of a sudden? They had both liked the little guy, she was sure. Victor wouldn't have worked that hard and that happily, building the little house. Lulu had been just as fond of him, giving him that cute name so he would fit into her family.

"Uh, thanks," Immy said. "I'm sure Drew will be very happy."

But would Ralph be happy? She wished she hadn't returned here for her charger. She could have bought another one. She really, really wished she had. She hoped Ralph would be glad to see her, but she wouldn't predict what he would do about this. She really did put him through a lot.

Thirty-One

A BIGGER QUESTION FOR IMMY WAS, could she finish working on her Case from Saltlick? Or would she have to return to Slap Out? She didn't have to check out of Motel Four since she had only paid for one night. After she had been on the road for a bit, headed toward Saltlick, she decided she absolutely had to call Ralph and tell him about Babalu. She had to warn him. She couldn't just spring Babalu on him. He might not go for having a goat, even though he had no objection to Marshmallow, and a pig was a lot more bother, Immy thought.

Babalu made his presence known, bleating with such a sharp sound it hurt Immy's ears. Maybe he would cry for a day, like a new kitten or puppy. If only it was an adult, she could stand that. Really, she should have asked Lulu or Victor what they did when they first got him, but she didn't especially want to talk to them again.

She plugged her phone in and pulled over to look at it, leaving the engine running to charge it. Oh no! Five calls from Ralph. Taking a deep breath, steeling herself, she called him.

"Immy? Hey, are you okay? I've been calling you."

"Uh, yeah, I'm okay. Are you? My phone ran out of battery." She pulled over to talk.

"I'm sorry for the way I acted. That wasn't fair. You worked hard for that certificate and I should be proud you actually got a job with it."

Yes, he should be. She bit her lower lip to keep from saying that. She got out of the car before Babalu started up again. He was so loud!

"I couldn't take any more time off work, so I had to go, but I didn't have to be so rude about it. You forgive me?"

"I guess. I don't know why you got so mad. I'm not in competition with you." She had parked at the side of the road in full sunshine and the car was heating up. To not suffocate her and the goat, she had had to roll down a window. It lessened the noise, too. Babalu was still carrying on back there in the crate. Did you crate a new goat like you did a new dog? She hoped there were answers online.

"Huh? I never thought you were, Immy. I'm just afraid you'll get hurt. What's all that noise?"

"It's the highway. I'm in my car." She had to tell him about the goat. He could clearly be heard with the windows down and she didn't dare go too far away.

"At least you're staying somewhere safe. Just promise me you'll think twice about everything you do. Don't be alone with anyone."

"I can promise you that."

"Say hi to Lulu and Victor for me. They seemed like nice folks."

"They did. But Victor has been getting drunk. There was a funeral for both of the dead guys and he's really upset by it. He seems to hate both of them. He doesn't even want to keep the goat that Long Tuttle gave them, just because it reminds him of Long."

"How angry is he?"

"He's...huh."

"Is he angry enough to have killed them?"

"You know, he was swindled out of his oil rights too, pretty recently, and that upset him a lot. Wyatt told me he was just as mad as everyone else."

"Be careful, Immy. Maybe you should stay somewhere else."

Yes, she should. And she had done that, and was checked out now.

"Love you, Immy. Come home soon."

"Love you too, Ralph. Say hi to Mother and Drew."

Now what? Maybe she shouldn't have taken the goat. She definitely had to head for home now. And she definitely should have told Ralph about the goat. They had gotten onto another subject and she hadn't been able to find a way to bring it up. He also distracted her. That was her excuse.

She got back on the road long enough to get to a rest area and pulled into it. She opened all the windows for ventilation for Babalu. What was she going to do? She couldn't keep the goat in the van all day and all night. It had to have a place.

She pondered the recent events. Lulu and Victor watching the report of Long's death on television. The room smelling of sulfur just after Long had been killed. Had Victor been in the oil field? Had he killed Long? Lulu had linked the two dead people together when she was talking about Babalu, about getting rid of some kind of reminder. The murders were surely linked, but how?

The morning of the wedding, Lulu had arrived at the church before Victor did. Could he have killed Junior? Maybe. She had to check that out. She had to go back. She would tell Lulu and Victor that she had to stay another day and ask them to keep the goat in their yard. She wouldn't stay in the house very long.

To turn around, she had to drive to the next exit ramp. She needed gas, so she pulled into a service station. Babalu looked hot. He shouldn't have to eat yet, but he was probably thirsty. If he drank, would he pee in her van? Her mother's van. Even worse.

His cries had softened, and for that she was thankful. Now they were pitiful little mews. Would he ramp the commotion back up or not?

She gassed up, then hurried back to Slap Out. She pulled up into the Henrys' driveway. Both cars were there. Because it was a warm day, some of the windows were open and she could hear raised voices.

Pausing at the bottom of the porch steps, she eavesdropped.

"If you hadn't gotten the wrong one in the first place, Vic." Lulu sounded angrier than Immy had ever heard her sound.

"They look exactly alike in the dark. How was I supposed to know? What the hell was the kid doing out there anyway?" Victor was slurring. Still drunk. Probably more drunk.

Immy thought fast. What was she hearing? Lulu had mentioned "the wrong one." The son instead of the father. Were her surmises hitting the mark?

"So you just followed the car and didn't know who was in it? And you never saw Long at all?" Immy imagined Lulu standing over him and shouting.

"How was I supposed to know he'd been there?" And Victor cowering at the table clutching a drink.

Long had known something, seen something? He had seen Victor kill Junior?

Immy couldn't stand up anymore. Her knees felt fragile, and her legs couldn't hold her up. She had to sit on a step. The smell of sulfur had been the clue. She had almost picked up on it. She had been just about to. Now, she had better get out of there.

She got back into her car and rolled up the windows, then called the police station and told them everything she had just heard.

Officer Powell answered. "You sure that's exactly what he said?"

"Yes, I just heard him. Just now. I'm right outside their house."

Officer Powell called out, "Hey chief, you know that set of prints that don't match anyone? I got somebody for you to try." Then he got back to Immy. "You stay outta that house. We're sending someone over right now."

She pulled the van out of the driveway and parked it on the opposite side of the street and down a house. This, she had to see. She got her newly charged phone ready to take pictures.

Within minutes two cars pulled up and Officer Powell and a female officer got out of the first car. Two others got out of the other car and went around to the backyard.

Hands on their holsters, the first two stomped up the steps and pounded on the door. "Police, open up!" said Powell.

Lulu opened it and stuck her head out. Immy could just barely see her from the angle of the vantage point she had. There was some quiet discussion. Before anything else could happen, the police from the second car came around front, holding Victor, handcuffed.

"Victor!" Lulu started screaming. "Victor, you have to tell them. You didn't do it. He didn't do it!"

Instead, he called back to her. "Take care of the pups!"

Immy followed the two cars to the police station and went inside. They were fingerprinting Victor. Officer Powell glared at her when she was two steps inside, so she left.

Thirty-Two

LULU WAS STILL BACK AT THE HOUSE, where the police had left her. She should probably have been arrested, too. All of her other assumptions were true, it seemed. The one about this being a job for two people was probably also true. Immy was glad she hadn't gone very far inside the station. That would be too close to Victor, the killer. She never wanted to see these people again.

Now it was finally time to go home.

Babalu was still making a racket, but he seemed quieter than he had been. As she got into the van, her cell rang. She didn't recognize the number, but thought maybe she should answer it. Maybe the police had some questions she could help clear up.

"Immy? Can you come to the house?"

It was Lulu! Lulu Henry! She didn't sound angry anymore. Immy could tell she was crying. Maybe she wasn't also guilty. Maybe it was just Victor. Should she go back there?

"Please? There's something I need to give you."

What could that possibly be? Immy had to know. Ralph had often told her that her curiosity would kill her, but Immy always told him it only killed cats, and anyway, they had nine lives.

"I can be there in a few minutes. I'm not very close." If Lulu hadn't seen her at their house, she wouldn't know how close Immy was. She could be in Ant Bite, for all Lulu knew.

She waited in the van, trying to talk to Babalu in soothing tones, but the goat probably couldn't even hear her over the racket he was setting up. He had resumed full volume when she got into the vehicle. All she could manage was fifteen minutes, then she got impatient and started the engine to drive the few minutes to the Henrys'. Maybe she could ask Lulu how she could comfort the goat. Although Lulu had turned on the animal and didn't want anything to do with him. Maybe she wouldn't ask her that.

Parking behind the two vehicles now in the drive, she got out and climbed the steps to the front door. It opened as she approached and Lulu smiled at her. Really? She was smiling? Immy thought she should act like she didn't know Victor had been arrested.

She tried to smile back. Maybe she succeeded. "Hi, how's it going? I was just about to leave town."

"I thought you left a while ago." Lulu motioned her inside, then closed the door and leaned against it with her hands behind her back.

They faced each other in the small front hall. "There were a few things I had to do."

"A few things? Like turn us in to the police?"

"What? Someone turned you in? What for? Where's Victor?"

Her smile was still there but it was pretty ugly now. Nothing like a moment ago. "Don't act cute. I saw you sitting there in that ugly van of yours when the cops came. And do you think I wouldn't hear the racket that damn goat was making?"

True, he had been loud the whole time. Immy was almost getting used to the din. "Well, it's my mother's van. But you're right, I did see the cops come to your house. I didn't want to mention it. What were they doing here?"

"I told you, don't act cute." She took her hands from behind her back and one of them was holding an old-time revolver. Probably from the 1950s, to match the rest of her life. "You're the official PI, right? You found out we killed those two monsters. You're the reason the cops came and got Victor."

"Is…is that a Colt?" Immy stared at the revolver. "Is it old?" Maybe it was old. Maybe it didn't work anymore.

"Don't worry, it still works just fine." Was the woman reading her mind?

"Are you sure? When's the last time you fired it?"

"Shut up! Shut up and march into the guest room! Right now!"

"Where are the dogs?" She didn't see or hear any sign of them.

"I said, shut up!"

Maybe Lulu didn't want to risk hurting them when she shot Immy, so had put them outside. That woman did love her dogs.

Immy started heading for the guest room, slowly. "You know, there's something I wanted to ask you about."

"Oh, you don't know exactly how we killed them? You think I would tell you that? So you can run to the cops and tell them everything?"

If only her phone were recording all of this. But it wasn't and there was no unobtrusive way to get it to do that now. "No, I wanted to ask you about a picture I found in the dresser. Is it a photo of little Davey?"

Immy heard the heavy gasp behind her. "What do you know about our son?"

Their son? It was time to start guessing. She wanted to keep the woman talking as long as possible, while she figured out what to do. "Nothing. I just know I heard you mention little Davey, and I saw a picture of a darling little boy in the drawer. I wondered if I was putting two and two together the right way."

She allowed herself to turn her head and saw Lulu slump, inadvertently lowering the pistol. Immy couldn't waste this moment.

She turned and grabbed the barrel. Lulu perked up and jerked on it with both hands, trying to aim it at Immy's midsection. They wrestled for what seemed like an hour to Immy, then she was able to twist the gun out of Lulu's hands.

Immy pushed Lulu aside and made a break for the front door. Four dogs were standing in a row, so that she would have to jump over them to get out.

Changing her plan in case they might jump and trip her (a good PI has to be flexible), she ran for the back door. Lulu wasn't far behind, though. She could hear her pounding footsteps and the dogs scampering after her.

Immy faced her, thinking she could make Lulu halt by aiming the gun at her. But Lulu had grabbed a huge shotgun from somewhere and was aiming that long, lethal barrel at her. Immy knew that Lulu was unlikely to miss, with the scattershot it was probably filled with. Did Immy dare to shoot Lulu? It was the last thing on earth she wanted to do. To shoot someone.

She fled. She was able to get through the gate and run into the oil field. There weren't many hiding places, but there were a few.

Why had she gone out the back door? She could have jumped over those dogs. They were all pretty short.

Running full tilt, she could hear the dogs yapping behind her, like she was a rabbit, or a fox, or maybe a raccoon, and they were hunting her.

The pumps, lined up like giant orderly insects, serenely stroked up and down in a long line. She ducked behind the large metal base of one. If it had just been Lulu, she could have hidden, but those dogs found her right away.

Running again, she heard buckshot whizzing past her. It was going awfully wide of the mark, from the dirt it was kicking up around her. Maybe Lulu was a bad enough shot that she wouldn't hit her after all. Running had to affect a person's aim. Immy turned her head and shoulders and fired from the revolver, aiming at the ground between them. She really didn't want to kill Lulu.

How many shells did the rifle have in it? Was it even a rifle? A shotgun? For that matter, how many bullets were in the revolver?

The one shot behind her seemed to have slowed Lulu down. When Immy got to the next pump, she ducked behind the base and peeked out to see where Lulu and the dogs were.

Lulu had stopped running. "Lucy! Ricky!" The dogs were ignoring her and coming after Immy. Lulu must have feared for them and was trying to call them to her. "Ethel! Phreddie!" One of the basset hounds stopped and looked back at his mistress, but then continued after his pack.

Immy didn't think she had to fear the dogs. In fact, with them between her and Lulu, she was probably safe from getting shot. But what would happen when the dogs reached her? Did she have time? She dialed 911.

"Nine one one, what is your emergency?"

"It's Immy Duckworthy. I'm in the oil field behind the Henrys' and Lulu is chasing me and shooting at me."

"Dispatch is on the way. Can you stay on the line?"

"I don't know."

The first two dogs reached her, the Corgi and the pug. She scooted away from them, tried to soothingly say their names in dog/baby talk. "Lucy, Ricky, you don't want to hurt me, right? You should go back to your house, right?"

They ignored her words and leaped on her, licking her face and arms. Oh great, they would subdue her with their tongues and their slobber.

Lulu would be here soon. Sooner than any cop could get here. If Lulu killed her, at least the woman would get arrested and go to prison for it. Immy would not have died in vain.

In a half a minute or so, Lulu appeared, rushing around the corner of the pump base. The bassets were at her heels and the Corgi and pug quit licking Immy and ran at Lulu, jumping on her joyously.

They succeeded in knocking her into the bassets, so that she fell to the ground.

Immy leapt at her and clutched the barrel of the shotgun. It was hot! But she didn't let go. She was able to pull it from Lulu and transfer her hold to the stock.

She was standing over Lulu with both firearms when the police showed up. One was the familiar, very tall Office Powell, and another one trailed behind him.

At first the other, younger cop aimed his weapon at Immy.

"No," Officer Powell told him. "I'm pretty sure this is the one we need to arrest." He pointed at Lulu, still sprawled on the dirt.

Immy wanted to pipe up and agree, but decided to hold her tongue. They were on the right track. She didn't want to distract them.

The other cop handcuffed Lulu and led her away, reading her rights to her. Officer Powell tried to catch the collars of the dogs. Immy grabbed two of them. They were surprisingly docile about their mistress being led away. But then, Lulu had taken it in stride. It was like she had expected it, by then.

"Officer Powell, I have a question."

He looked a little weary, but raised his eyebrows to receive her query.

"Who was Davey? Did the Henrys have a child named Davey?"

He looked at the ground and shook his head. "That's a sad story. He was swimming at the city pool, wasn't more than five or so. He couldn't swim and he got into the deep end. The kid on lifeguard duty had left to grab a smoke and the little boy drowned."

"That's…awful. Who was the lifeguard?"

"Ned Newberry, Jr."

So the Henrys had more than one problem with the Newberrys, this problem with Junior, specifically. Maybe he hadn't been shot by accident, in place of his father, as Lulu had thought.

"Do you want to take these?" She managed to hold both weapons out without losing hold of the dogs. "They belong to Lulu. Or Victor. Anyway, they're not mine."

"Good work, then. Getting both of them away from her."

"Yeah, she was pretty determined to kill me. She told me they both murdered the two young men, her and Victor, not just Victor. Then, I guess, she felt she had to get rid of me after she told me that."

"We've been talking to Victor and were probably going to come arrest Lulu tomorrow."

"He blabbed?"

"He implicated his wife."

Immy shook her head. "Someone should take care of these dogs. They saved my life."

"Do you want them?"

"No!"

"We'll find them a home. I don't think that'll be hard."

Then Immy made her way slowly to the street, where the car, her mother's van, was parked.

As soon as she climbed inside, she locked all the doors. Babalu was still complaining loudly.

*****

Stopping only to give Babalu some water halfway there, from a cup she got at a drive-through, she drove straight home. It was just getting dark when she arrived at Ralph's. Hers and Ralph's. Where she now lived. If he hadn't decided to kick her out.

When she pulled up he dashed out. Only then did she realize she hadn't actually warned him about the goat. She had meant to. But then they had talked and she had decided she knew who the killer was.

When she opened the door and jumped out, Ralph backed up a couple of steps. "What's that smell?" he asked.

"Oh, that? It's the, uh, goat." She glanced nervously at the back of the van.

Drew had followed him out by now. "Goat? What goat? You got me a goat?"

"It's Babalu, sweetie. The Henrys had to get rid of him."

"So they got arrested? Both of them?" Maybe she could keep Ralph talking about this instead of the goat.

"Eventually. First they arrested Victor, then Lulu chased me and tried to kill me. I called nine one one when I was hiding in the oil field, and they managed to get her before she did it.

Ralph considered. "I guess they couldn't keep the goat then, if they're both maybe going to jail. To prison. But there's no one in the town who can keep a goat?" Nope, he was back on the subject of goats.

"I didn't ask. The Henrys wanted me to have it. That was before I knew them, you know." She didn't want to use the words "kill" and "murder" in front of her daughter.

"The arrested alleged murderers wanted that. And you bow to the wishes of felons. Does that make sense?" Ralph didn't understand about not using those words.

She was going to have to talk to him about the goat. She hadn't been going to, but she told him she'd decided to bring Babalu home before the police came and got them. "Lulu said she wanted me to have him, to get rid of him. Probably because she killed Long, the guy who gave the goat to her."

"What is wrong with you, Immy? Seriously, what is wrong with you?"

"Ralph Sandoval, you're lucky I didn't bring four dogs back with me, too."

By this time Drew had thrown open the van doors and was working to open the cage. Maybe she hadn't paid attention to what words they were using.

"Wait!" Immy didn't think they should let Babalu run loose in the front yard. "Let's get him to the backyard first."

Ralph gave her a dirty look, then lifted the cage out of the van and carried it on one shoulder to the fenced-in backyard. Immy's heart sped up a little watching his bulging muscles as he carried that heavy, awkward weight.

He came back to the van for the stuff to feed Babalu. When Drew came into the backyard, the goat started cavorting immediately. Running, jumping straight up, kicking, bleating. Although Drew couldn't kick her hind legs the way he did, since she only had two of them, she could bleat well. Immy hardly noticed his eyes anymore.

Ralph disappeared into the house as she watched the joy of her daughter, and of the little goat. Marshmallow decided to sit it out. He went to the corner of the yard and watched from there.

"Drew, let's introduce Babalu to Marshmallow, okay?"

"Okay!" She ran to her pig and hugged him.

Immy grabbed the little goat around his neck, and reached for the collar that was buried deep in his fur, held onto that and persuaded him to come with her. She would have to get a leash. Long had had him one. When they got to the pig, Immy tried to get their noses together, but maybe that worked better with dogs. Marshmallow swung his big head away and Babalu tried to butt him.

"No, bad goat!" Drew shoved Babalu away.

"Let's introduce them gradually," Immy said. "Why don't you take Marshmallow inside and I'll stay here with this little guy for a little while. When he settles down a bit, I think I should feed him."

Drew led Marshmallow up the ramp Ralph had built for him when they first came to live there.

Eventually, after observing Babalu's manic, hilarious antics for a few minutes, Immy fed and watered the goat, zipping inside to get an old metal bowl she didn't think anyone would need. She hoped it wouldn't turn out to be Ralph's favorite bowl. When Babalu finished vacuuming up his hay and lapping his water, he butted the water bowl until it was upside down. It was dented now, so it wouldn't be anyone's favorite, if it had been.

"See you later, little fella." Immy went inside to see how Ralph was feeling.

Her mother and Drew were in the kitchen making cookies. Marshmallow was hanging around near them in hopes they would drop some of the ingredients. He was probably correct in those hopes. At least Drew probably would.

"Salutations, Imogene. I will be removing myself to my own domicile as soon as these baked goods go into the oven. Please listen for the timer and take them out."

"Sure, I can do that. Is Ralph still here?" she asked.

Her mother nodded toward the door into the living room. When she came into the room, he got up from his favorite ratty chair and went out the front door. The television was playing the news, so she glanced at it and found it was supposed to rain the next day. Nothing else seemed to be important enough to broadcast, since they dwelt on that for a good long time.

"Imogene, I want to make you aware of a happenstance. It might and might not become a happenstance, in reality. I heard from my cousin, Ouida, this afternoon."

"How is she doing? She was in bad shape when I was there. And she was all alone, as far as I could tell."

"That was true, most likely. Her spouse has vacated their premises and has decided to domicile with his nubile, young secretary."

"Oh no! On top of everything else! The poor woman." Maybe Lulu and Victor should have killed both the men in that family. No, she hadn't just thought that, had she? She shouldn't have.

"Yes, indeed, the poor woman. I have offered my premises and she has agreed to share my abode with me for an indeterminate amount of time."

"Your premises. Okay." Immy wasn't at all sure how that would work. "That's awfully nice of you, Mother."

Hortense didn't answer the compliment, but took up her purse and went out the front door, telling Drew to watch the cookies in the oven.

After what Immy thought might be an appropriate interval, a few minutes after her mother had left, she joined Ralph on the porch.

"Immy, what were you thinking? You brought a goat to my house without asking me?"

"Our house, I thought."

"It's our house while I let you live here."

"That's not fair. Drew and I have moved in. We're living here. All my stuff is here."

He looked away and didn't reply.

"That little goat is awfully cute. Drew loves him."

"Goats smell bad. They chew everything."

"I can sell him if you want."

He turned to look at her. "You can't sell it now. You'll break Drew's heart. She loves it."

"Him, it's a him. So you're okay with keeping him?"

"I'm not okay! I'm over a barrel. We can't get rid of it because of Drew."

That was true, Immy knew. She also knew she should have warned him. Or, maybe, asked him.

"Get rid of him. Hey, I'm sorry. I meant to tell you when I called, then we talked about other things and I forgot. I thought it would be okay. I mean, you have a pig in the house."

"I always knew Marshmallow was coming. See the difference? We talked about that. I had plenty of time to get used to him."

So Marshmallow was a "him" and Babalu was merely an "it." Immy hung her head, exasperated. She wondered how long it would take for Ralph to get over this, to learn to like, maybe even love, Babalu, and forget about this argument. He had a big heart. It would open for the adorable goat, she was sure. But how long would that take?

"Do you want to hear about the Case?"

"We talked about it on the phone. On your way here. With a goat in the van."

Drew called from inside. "Mommy! Hurry! The cookies!"

She ran in to take them from the oven, just before they burned. Since they were her mother's cookies, she had to have one, fresh off the baking sheet.

As she was taking the cookies off the sheet, her legs started itching. Within minutes, they were on fire. When she got the cookies taken care of, she looked down.

Poison ivy. She had crouched in poison ivy in the oil field. She had that rash. Again. At least there was calamine lotion in the medicine cabinet. Rubbing it onto her bumpy legs, she wondered if Lulu had it too, in jail.

Ralph didn't forget about their quarrel that night. She had thought some cookies would soften him, but they didn't. He slept on his side of the bed with his back to her, near the edge. There was not even a goodnight kiss. In the morning, he got up, showered and dressed, and left for work without a word. Immy assumed he would get breakfast somewhere else.

She hadn't even told him about her escapade and her escape from Lulu and death.

Drew soon came into the bedroom and urged her mom to get up and fix her something to eat. "I think the cookies are still good."

Immy smiled. "You can't have cookies for breakfast. Later, you can have some."

"Would Babalu like them?"

"I'm sure he would."

"Marshmallow likes them."

"Don't feed very many cookies to either of them. That's not what they're supposed to eat."

"But little girls are s'pose to, right?"

"Yes, they definitely are. After they have had their breakfast."

Drew cheered her up and almost made her forget about how upset Ralph was. Almost, but not quite.

Thirty-Three

After all the humans and animals had eaten, Immy unpacked and set up her laptop to email a bill to Eccles Justice. She called it an invoice, since that sounded more professional. She figured now was a good time, since he wasn't a suspect anymore. In the invoice, she explained how she uncovered evidence against the Henrys so he would know she had earned it. Tentatively, she added mileage to her expenses. To Hillstown and Ant Bite. But she didn't label them, just gave the figures.

She wasn't sure the Case was completely over or that it was time for her to be paid. Or that she even would be paid. This being her first case and all, she had been winging it so far, so she might as well keep winging it.

She puttered around for a bit on the computer, looking at this and that on the Internet, then heard a ding. Clicking over to her payment app, she found she had just been paid. Already. She hadn't had to talk him into it, like she expected she might have to. Her payment wasn't in the amount she had billed him for. It was quite a bit more! There was a "thank you" comment attached.

Wow! Sitting back in her chair, which was Ralph's old ratty chair, she smiled bigger than she had for quite a while. So, it *was* time for her to be paid. The Case *was* over. Maybe she would rest on her laurels for just a bit.

Drew ran in from the yard and asked to go to the park with the goat.

Immy had to explain that Babalu couldn't go with them, saying there was a policy at the park about goats (there should have been, after all), but Drew wanted to go anyway. So they drove there and started walking around the lake. Saltlick had a small park on the edge of town. It was mostly soccer fields, tennis and basketball courts, and a baseball diamond, but there was a swing set and a slide.

Drew didn't say anything about there not being a sign forbidding goats, luckily. While Immy was pushing Drew, trying to encourage her to pump herself—Immy knew she could do that if she wanted to—a migrating flock of noisy geese flew overhead. Drew squealed in delight at the racket of the honking. Immy always loved that sound, for some reason.

When they got back, Hortense called and invited them all for dinner. Ralph was home, so she ran it past him and he was glad to go. That was no surprise. He had never turned down Hortense's cooking.

They came in, bearing a bouquet of carnations and a bottle of wine, but Hortense didn't greet them. Ouida Newberry did. Immy had forgotten she was staying there.

"Oh, hi. Ralph, do you know Mrs. Newberry? She's Mother's cousin, from Slap Out."

"Ouida, please. Glad to meet you, Ralph."

"Same here, ma'am. How are you finding Saltlick?"

"I haven't been out much. Mostly just staying in with my cousin. It was so nice of her to have me. I couldn't stay in that house another minute."

She seemed like a completely different person, completely normal.

Hortense was still in the kitchen, but she came out and caught the end of what her cousin was saying. "It's fine, Ouida. You know you can stay her. Stay as long as you have to."

Immy noticed her mother didn't invite the woman to stay as long as she liked, only as long as she had to. She wondered if her mother might be getting tired of the house guest.

"Please, find a seat everyone. Ouida and I can serve you."

Ouida brought out a serving bowl of salad and handed it to Immy to pass around.

When it got to Drew, she stared at the bowl. "Why is there only one piece of tomato?" Drew loved tomatoes.

Hortense walked in with a water pitcher, set it on the table, and came over to Drew's chair. "One tomato? I put a lot of pieces in the salad." Hortense looked at her cousin. "Ouida, do you know what happened to the tomatoes?"

The woman shrugged, not looking at Hortense.

Immy stared at her. So, not so normal, after all. Had she really eaten all the tomatoes out of the salad? If she had, it was a mistake leaving one piece there, all by itself.

Ouida spoke then. "Do you want me to get the rest of the meal?"

"No thank you. Definitely not. You stay right there. I will serve the rest of the repast."

The meal went well from there, pork chops, mashed potatoes with Hortense's heavenly gravy, and fresh-cooked green beans with butter and dill weed.

Conversation centered on the weather and the upcoming high school football season, and the missing tomatoes were forgotten. Well, not forgotten, but not mentioned again.

When everyone had finished, Ouida jumped up and said she would clear.

"I'll help you." Hortense joined her and they whisked the empty plates away. No one had left a morsel on their dishes.

Immy was relieved that the tomato incident was over. Until Hortense screamed in the kitchen.

"What did you do? How could you?"

Ouida came out of the kitchen and departed to the bedroom she was using, the one that used to be Immy's.

Immy ran to the kitchen. "What's wrong? What happened?"

"Look!" Hortense was still screeching. "Look at these cupcakes!"

Two dozen chocolate cupcakes sat on a serving platter. A little more than half of them were beautifully frosted. The rest…were not. There were slight, faint traces of icing on those.

"Did someone…lick these?"

Hortense was fuming too much to answer. She picked up all of the cupcakes that were bereft of frosting and threw them into the trash. "I can't. You take these out, please, to Ralph and Drew."

She did as her mother bade her to do and set the cupcakes between Ralph and Drew.

Ralph gave her a questioning look. "They look fine," he whispered. "What happened?"

Immy whispered back, on the side away from Drew, so she wouldn't hear. "She licked the frosting off some of them."

Unfortunately, Drew's hearing was excellent. "Licked off the frosting?"

"Shush. Let's not talk about it. Okay? Maybe later. Not now." Immy took one and sat to peel off the paper and enjoy it as best she could, with the tension floating around the singlewide so thick you could almost see it. Hortense stayed in the kitchen.

When they had each eaten one, Immy took them back to the kitchen. "I think we had better leave. Thanks so much, Mother. Everything was delicious. As always."

She was shocked to see tear tracks on her mother's cheeks.

"I can't, Imogene. I want to be charitable and she is family. But I don't think I am capable of assisting this woman."

"Do you want me to tell her to find someplace else? I can do it if you want me to." Immy knew she, herself, would use language that Ouida would understand. She might not comprehend her mother's convoluted verbiage.

Hortense heaved a huge sigh, her ample bosom rising and falling a few inches. "No, I must do it. You go on home. Thank you for your invaluable presence tonight."

Immy hugged her mother and was rewarded with a warm reciprocal embrace.

She worried about her mother, dealing with that cousin. Ouida was either still deranged from grief, or her husband's leaving, or she was just plain rude. Was she always like that? At any rate, they needed to find another place for her to stay. She couldn't stay with Hortense, no matter how big-hearted Hortense was trying to be.

Then there was the surprise goat. The surprise to Ralph.

Through the week, Ralph gradually thawed, but there was no discussion about Babalu. Would he cave in gradually, bit by bit? Maybe, Immy thought, she should just let it go, like the water that raced down over the fake rocks at the Wymee Falls and disappeared into the river. That went against her grain, though. She wanted to struggle upriver, as it were, and talk this out. But they were speaking civilly to each other now, at least, and the atmosphere was nicer than it had been a few days ago. She told herself this wasn't because Ralph was so shallow that he was impressed with her paycheck. He had said so. That pleased her no end, she had to admit. But the thawing, she had to believe, was something that would have happened anyway, paycheck or not.

She consulted with him about a workable desk for herself and they finally decided to move the furniture a bit—it didn't take much—so that she had a space in the corner of the living room. The television was also there, but she could work mostly during the day when Ralph was at work. It was in the evenings that he very much liked to watch the news and weather. And sports. Immy was quite optimistic this would work out. With her earnings, she got herself the small desk she wanted and a nice chair. And even a filing cabinet, a wooden one instead of a metal one, to make the room not look too much like a police station, which she thought a metal one might do.

She called her mother every evening and there was no change. Ouida was still there, and still wandering around the trailer, clueless, getting into things. Mostly food. She was such a tiny thing and she only took tiny bites out of things. But those tiny bites ruined the things she bit. Hortense told her daughter that she had made a soufflé and had planned to bring it to them, but Ouida started poking it with a fork and it fell flat. Hortense scooped some out on a plate for Ouida and some for herself, and threw the rest into the trash.

"Imogene, I am wasting an inordinate amount of food this week."

"Mother, this can't continue. I saw that the church is having a singles gathering tomorrow night. Maybe you could both go to that and you could find someone to take her off your hands."

"Foist her off on a prospective suitor? That doesn't seem, well, suitable."

"Mother, it's past time to worry about niceties. Do you want me to go with you?"

"When is it?"

"Wednesday, tomorrow night."

It was decided that Hortense would escort Ouida there, and they would see where the chips fell. Immy's phrase, not Hortense's.

Thirty-Four

THURSDAY MORNING ORTENSE CALLED HER DAUGHTER.

"Imogene, your idea was inspired. It worked beautifully."

"She's hooking up with someone?"

"I'm not sure that would be the proper term, but she is packing to move in with Mr. Yarborough."

Immy was speechless. "She's hooking up with a Yarborough?" The Yarborough twins were the chief troublemakers in Saltlick.

"This is a distant relation. Phil Yarborough, he said. He's just moved to Wymee Falls from Houston. From my perspective, he appeared presentable. His table manners are impeccable, and it is hoped he can instill them into Ouida."

"But they're moving in together, just like that?"

"I believe she felt that we should no longer domicile together. She feels that way as much as I do, or many even more so. She is a grown woman and this is her choice."

"Does he know what's happened to her? All the baggage she's dealing with?"

"The issues were addressed by her, to him, and he listened intently. He seems determined to help out the poor woman. He recently lost his wife to cancer and would very much like companionship."

"Mother, you were determined to help her out, too."

Immy heard her mother sniff. "The matter is closed. If she needs another place to stay, I shall endeavor to find one for her."

"But not your place."

"Definitely not."

*****

The Wednesday of the next week Immy got an email from her client. Her former client, more correctly, since their contract was over. Mr. Justice told Immy, in case she was interested, that there would be a hearing for the Henrys and formal charges would be made on Friday.

To her utter surprise, Ralph wasn't against her going back to that part of Texas to see this. The hearing would be in Hillstown, where the county courthouse was, so they wouldn't be in Slap Out, which was good. But Ralph suggested Drew stay in Saltlick with her Geemaw and he would drive there with Immy.

She turned this over in her mind. Did he think she needed protecting? Or was he just finally curious about her Case? Either way, she would be glad to have the company. Her acceptance was enthusiastic, after bowing her head and thinking it through for three or four seconds.

The next Friday came in no time. They left early in the morning and would drive back the same day. Immy never wanted to stay at Motel Four again and her other lodgings were completely unavailable. She didn't know what was happening at the Henrys' cute house, and didn't really want to know. There were places to stay in Hillstown, she was sure, but they would be more expensive, it being a bigger city. They made good time on the road and walked into the courthouse just before the hearing was scheduled to begin.

They each pulled down a wooden fold-up seat and sat in the back. It wasn't long before the two subjects were led to the tables in the front of the room. So, it appeared that they were both going to be charged together.

Immy got a glimpse of their stoic faces before they took seats next to their lawyer with their backs to the room. Both Lulu and Victor looked small in the rather large courtroom in Hillstown, the county seat for Slap Out and the surrounding area. She and Ralph were conspicuous since there weren't many other people there. Victor glared at her whenever he could manage to glance over his shoulder.

As the legalese was read, Immy admired the tall, skinny, windows at the front of the room, with colored inserts and the beautiful wood flooring. It made for a lovely room, though it echoed from the hard surfaces.

Halfway through the proceedings, Eccles Justice walked in, alone, and sat on their row, a few seats away. He removed his hat as he sat and Immy noticed a new feather, longer than the one he had lost.

The couple were charged with the murders, Victor as the killer and Lulu as an accomplice. Immy thought maybe all that Lulu did was to keep quiet about it and not turn in her husband, but that was enough for the law. She wondered if that was right, or if Lulu was the killer and Victor was the accomplice. She also wondered how the dogs were doing, but there was no one to ask except Eccles. She didn't want to bother him with that. And she certainly wasn't going to take them home with her. Ralph would throw her out, for sure.

Bail was set fairly high and they were taken away in handcuffs. Immy wondered if they would make the bail. She was glad they didn't know exactly where she lived.

Eccles greeted her warmly as everyone was leaving. That was appropriate, she had to admit, since Immy had freed him of suspicion. But she wished he could be made to pay for his other crimes. He wasn't a model citizen. Or even a good person.

On the way home she suggested stopping in Slap Out, but Ralph refused. That was probably better. If they went there, she would want to see Wyatt and Sydney and check up on them and that might be inappropriate. Also, someone might talk her into taking those adorable dogs.

Back home, the next week, at her office desk, while Ralph was at work and Drew was at preschool, she phoned Wyatt. He sounded pretty good. He said he and his father were thinking of moving to Dallas, where they had some relatives. They would be selling all of their land and just getting out of there. When she asked about the dogs, he said that Loryetta's family had taken them. So Eccles Justice and his daughter were doing something good.

Thirty-Five

IMMY WAS STILL ASLEEP WHEN HER MOTHER KNOCKED on the door. She only knew it was her mother after she heard Ralph, who had gotten up and was fixing breakfast, opened the front door and greeted her.

"Come to see the big day, Hortense?" he asked.

"I would not miss it for all of the tea in China, so to speak."

Her eyes flying open, Immy jumped out of bed. She should have gotten up early. She had almost forgotten! Ralph should have woken her up!

This was the day! This was Drew's first day of real school, kindergarten. The child had been so excited the night before that it had taken an extra hour of bedtime reading before she could fall asleep. Maybe that's why Immy was sleeping in today.

Immy emerged in time to see Drew come running to the front room. "Lookee me, Geemaw! I have a new dress!"

She said "dress" with an *R*. Her *R*s and *L*s had improved over the last year and she would be entering school without that impediment. Immy had worked on that, but Geemaw had worked harder.

"My goodness, you do, Nancy Drew. It's dazzling! My eyes are well-pleased. Who is going to fix your hair?"

Drew pouted. "I already fixed it. It's fixed."

"I believe we can titivate your appearance a bit before you go. Have you consumed breakfast yet?"

"Yep. Ate it all up."

"Very well. Come with me to the lavatory and we shall endeavor to make a few minor adjustments."

A few minutes later, Drew emerged with satin ribbons in her hair that, amazingly, matched her blue dress. Immy didn't know where they had come from, but she remembered that she had shown the dress to her mother a few days ago. Hortense had remembered the shade exactly. The model grandmother.

They all four rode in the van to drop her off. They waited their turn in the semicircular driveway, behind the other parents dropping the other children off for the very first day of school. When they reached the head of the line, Drew dashed out with her backpack of brand-new supplies after hasty kisses in the van. She didn't look back. Immy felt some deflation as they drove away. Hortense dropped them off back at their house, then Ralph drove off to work in his truck and Immy went inside to her home office.

Over the last year, since her first case in Slap Out, Immy had worked quite a few more of those cases and had even done some private investigating for Mike Mallett, her old boss, as a contractor. Most of her business came from Wymee Falls, but she'd looked into a few family problems in Saltlick, too.

Ouida had called Hortense regularly, reporting on her new life with Phil Yarborough. According to what she told Hortense, they were happy and in love. Immy wondered if her manners had improved, or if they even mattered, living with just one person. At any rate, Hortense was not responsible for her anymore, and never would be again. Hortense was adamant about that. Cousin or not.

Immy booted up her laptop and read over the local news from Hillstown, as she had been doing for a year, then stopped short at an article that leapt off the screen. The headline read: Local Couple Convicted in Double Slaying. It was her case! Her Case! The Henrys had both been found guilty, a mere year after they'd been arrested. Both of them! Avidly, she devoured the details. DNA and phone records had been their downfall. Those had placed them at the scenes at the right times. Well, the wrong times for them.

Immy was sorry that they had to leave the house they loved so much, and also their pets. But Victor had let anger eat him up, rule his life, and drive him into committing those horrible crimes. It was a shame, she thought. Even though the guys who died were not nice people, that wasn't the way to solve problems. That was never the way. They should have hired private investigators to dig up incriminating evidence. That would have been the right way.

A ping heralded an email hitting her inbox. It was coming from the contact form on her professional web page. It was, she was elated to see, an inquiry about hiring her to find out who was stealing a local farmer's calves. She didn't think that would be hard to solve. Some late-night stakeouts, setting up some cameras maybe.

After making note of these and a few more ideas, she answered the message and was on her way to her next Case. This one would be easy to name. She drew a folder from her desk drawer and labeled it with a marker. The Case to Catch the Calf Nabber.

About the Author

Kaye George is an award-winning novelist and short-story writer. She writes cozy and traditional mysteries, a prehistory series, and has a suspense novel coming out soon, which will be her seventeenth book. Over fifty short stories have been published, mostly in anthologies and magazines. With family scattered all over the globe, she makes her home in Knoxville TN.